Western titles by Ed Gorman

LYNCHED
RELENTLESS
VENDETTA
GHOST TOWN
LAWLESS
STORM RIDERS

Western titles edited by Ed Gorman and Martin H. Greenberg

STAGECOACH
GUNS OF THE WEST
DESPERADOES
THE BEST OF THE AMERICAN WEST
THE BEST OF THE AMERICAN WEST II

Stagecoach

Edited by
Ed Gorman
and **Martin H. Greenberg**

BERKLEY BOOKS, NEW YORK

This is a work of fiction. Names, characters, places, and incidents either are the product of the author's imagination or are used fictitiously, and any resemblance to actual persons, living or dead, business establishments, events, or locales is entirely coincidental.

STAGECOACH

A Berkley Book / published by arrangement with
the editors

PRINTING HISTORY
Berkley edition / September 2003

Copyright © 2003 by Ed Gorman.
A complete listing of the individual copyrights and permissions can be found on page 195.
Cover illustration by Guy Deel.
Cover design by Jill Boltin.

For information address: The Berkley Publishing Group,
a division of Penguin Group (USA) Inc.,
375 Hudson Street, New York, New York 10014.

ISBN: 0-425-19205-9

BERKLEY®
Berkley Books are published by The Berkley Publishing Group,
a division of Penguin Group (USA) Inc.,
375 Hudson Street, New York, New York 10014.
BERKLEY and the "B" design
are trademarks belonging to Penguin Group (USA) Inc.

PRINTED IN THE UNITED STATES OF AMERICA

10 9 8 7 6 5 4 3 2 1

Contents

Introduction

∽◦∾

While we often think of the stagecoach as a uniquely American conveyance, it began its life in the England of Queen Elizabeth the First. It was brought over to the early American colonies, where its use flourished. Sometime in the 1820s, stagecoaches began appearing on the western frontier. And the rest is legend. And lore.

The Concord, despite a lot of also-rans, began the standard by which all other stagecoaches were measured. And it was the Concord that was used by most writers of Western fiction and directors of Western movies.

Our collection opens with one of Louis L'Amour's most powerful stories, "Bluff Creek Station," a unique story about a station hostler, a man who runs a stop on the stage trail. A stop—food, water, rest—for horses and humans alike.

The other stories, by such well-known western writers as Richard S. Wheeler, Don Coldsmith, and Robert J. Conley, use the stage as a point of departure. A stage pulls into Tombstone . . . a passenger disembarks . . . and his or her story begins. Loren D. Estleman, Judy Alter, and Robert J. Randisi are among our other authors.

Of all the legends of the West, the stagecoach still stands tall, a dusty, dangerous mode of transportation that nonetheless inspired many, many additions to the romance of the Old (and mythic) West. We hope you enjoy these stories as much as we do.

—The Editors

Bluff Creek Station

～∾⌇∾～

by Louis L'Amour

Louis L'Amour (1908–1988) was the most successful Western writer of all time, selling 15,000–20,000 books a day at the height of his popularity. He wrote the kind of action fiction beloved by so many generations of Americans, with strong heroes, evil villains, proud, energetic heroines, and all of the excitement and danger that the West represented. His novels include such masterpieces as *Hondo, Shalako, Down the Long Hills, The Cherokee Trail,* and *Last of the Breed.* His most famous series was the Sacketts saga, later made into several excellent television movies. And yet, often overlooked in all his success was the humanistic side of L'Amour, as demonstrated in this wonderful story.

THE STAGE WAS two hours late into Bluff Creek and the station hostler had recovered his pain-wracked consciousness three times. After two futile attempts to move himself, he had given up and lay sprawled on the rough boards of the floor with a broken back and an ugly hole in his side.

He was a man of middle years, his jaw unshaved and his hair rumpled and streaked with gray. His soiled shirt and homespun jeans were dark with blood. There was one unlaced boot on his left foot. The other boot lay near a fireplace gray with ancient ashes.

There were two benches and a few scattered tools, some odd bits of harness, an overturned chair, and a table on which were some unwashed dishes. Near the hostler's right hand lay a Spencer rifle, and beyond it a double-barreled shotgun. On the floor nearby, within easy reach, a double row of neatly spaced shotgun and rifle shells. Scattered about were a number of used shells from both weapons, mute mementos of his four-hour battle with attacking Indians.

Now, for slightly more than two hours there had been no attack, yet he knew they were out there, awaiting the arrival of the stage, and it was for this he lived, to fire a warning shot before the stage could stop at the station. The last shot they fired, from a Sharps .50, had wrecked his spine. The bloody wound in his side had come earlier in the battle, and he had stuffed it with cotton torn from an old mattress.

Outside, gray clouds hung low, threatening rain, and occasional gusts of wind rattled the dried leaves on the trees, or stirred them along the hard ground.

The stage station squatted in dwarfish discomfort at the foot of a bluff, the station was constructed of blocks picked from the slide-rock at the foot of the bluff, and it was roofed with split cedar logs covered with earth. Two small windows stared in mute wonderment at the empty road and at the ragged brush before it where the Indians waited.

Three Indians, he believed, had died in the battle, and probably he had wounded as many more, but he distrusted counting Indian casualties, for all too often they were overestimated. And the Indians always carried away their dead.

The Indians wanted the stage, the horses that drew it, and the weapons of the people inside. There was no way to warn the driver or passengers unless he could do it. The hostler lay on his back staring up at the ceiling.

He had no family, and he was glad of that now. Ruby

had run off with a tinhorn from Alta some years back, and there had been no word from her, nor had he wished for it. Occasionally, he thought of her, but without animosity. He was not, he reminded himself, an easy man with whom to live, nor was he much of a person. He had been a simple, hardworking man, inclined to drink too much, and often quarrelsome when drinking.

He had no illusions. He knew he was finished. The heavy lead slug that had smashed the base of his spine had killed him. Only an iron will had kept life in his body, and he doubted his ability to keep it there much longer. His legs were already dead, and there was a coldness in his fingers that frightened him. He would need those fingers to fire the warning shot.

Slowly, carefully, he reached for the shotgun and loaded it with fumbling, clumsy fingers. Then he wedged the shotgun into place in the underpinning of his bunk. It was aimed at nothing, but all he needed was the shot, the dull boom it would make, a warning to those who rode the stage that something was amiss.

He managed to knot a string to the trigger so it could be pulled even if he could not reach the trigger. His extremities would go first, and then even if his fingers were useless, he could pull the trigger with his teeth.

Exhausted by his efforts, he lay back and stared up at the darkening ceiling, without bitterness; waiting for the high, piercing yell of the stage driver and the rumble and rattle of the stage's wheels as it approached the station.

Five miles east, the heavily loaded stage rolled along the dusty trail accompanied by its following plume of dust. The humped-up clouds hung low over the serrated ridges. Up on the box, Kickapoo Jackson handled the lines and beside him Hank Wells was riding shotgun. Wells was deadheading it home as there was nothing to guard coming west. He had his revolving shotgun and a rifle with him from force of habit. The third man who rode the top, lying between some sacks of mail, was Marshal Brad

Delaney, a former buffalo hunter and Indian fighter.

Inside the stage a stocky, handsome boy with brown hair sat beside a pretty girl in rumpled finery. Both looked tired and were, but the fact that they were recently married was written all over them. Half the way from Kansas City they had talked of their hopes and dreams, and their excitement had been infectious. They had enlisted the advice and sympathy of those atop the coach as well as those who rode inside.

The tall man of forty with hair already gray at the temples was Dr. Dave Moody, heading for the mining camps of Nevada to begin a new practice after several years of successful work in New England. Major Glen Faraday sat beside him at the window. Faraday was a West Point man, now discharged from the Army and en route west to build a flume for an irrigation project.

Ma Harrigan, who ran a boardinghouse in Austin and was reputed to make the best pies west of the Rockies, sat beside Johnny Ryan, headed west to the father he had never seen.

Kickapoo Jackson swung the Concord around a bend and headed into a narrow draw. "Never liked this place!" he shouted. "Too handy for injuns!"

"Seen any around?" Delaney asked.

"Nope! But the hostler at Bluff Creek had him a brush with them a while back. He driv 'em off, though! That's a good man, yonder!"

"That's his kid down below," Wells said. "Does he know the kid's comin' west?"

"Know?" Kickapoo spat. "Ryan don't even know he's got a kid! His wife run off with a no-account gambler a few years back! When the gambler found she was carryin' another man's child, he just up and left her. She hadn't known about the kid when she left Ryan."

"She never went back?"

"Too proud, I reckon. She waited tables in Kansas City a while, then got sickly. Reckon she died. The folks the boy lived with asked me to bring him back to his dad. Ol' Ryan will sure be surprised!"

The grade steepened, and Jackson slowed the stage for the long climb. Brad Delaney sat up and surveyed the sage-covered hills with a wary eye, cradling his Winchester on his knees. No chance of surprising them here despite their slow pace. Here the Indians would be in the open, which would mean suicide for them. Hank Wells was a seasoned fighting man, and there wasn't a better man with the ribbons than old Kickapoo.

Down inside they had Doc, who had fought in the War Between the States, and the major, who was a veteran soldier. The newly married kid handled a rifle like he knew what it was meant for, and unless they were completely surprised, any batch of raiders would run into trouble with this stage.

At Bluff Creek all was quiet. Dud Ryan stared up into the gathering darkness and waited. From time to time he could put an eye to a crack and study the road and the area beyond it. They were there . . . waiting.

Delaney and Wells would be riding the stage this trip, and they were canny men. Yet they would not be expecting trouble at the stage station. When they rolled into sight of it there would be a letdown, an easing-off, and the Indians would get off a volley before the men on the stage knew what hit them.

With Brad and Hank out of the picture, and possibly Kickapoo Jackson, the passengers could be slaughtered like so many mice. Caught inside the suddenly stalled stage, with only its flimsy sides to protect them, they would have no chance.

Only one thing remained. He must somehow remain alive to warn them. A warning shot would have them instantly alert, and Hank Wells would whip up his team and they would go through and past the station at a dead run. To warn them he must be alive.

Alive?

Well, he knew he was dying. He had known from the moment he took that large-caliber bullet in the spine. Without rancor he turned the idea over in his mind. Life hadn't given him much, after all. Yet dying wouldn't be so bad if he felt that his dying would do any good.

The trouble was, no man was ever ready to die. There was always something more to do, something undone, even if only to cross the street.

Behind him the years stretched empty and alone. Even the good years with Ruby looked bleak when he thought of them. He had never been able to give her anything, and maybe that was why he drank. Like all kids he had his share of dreams, and he was ready to take the world by the throat and shake it until it gave him the things he desired. Only stronger, more able men seemed always to get what he wanted. Their women had the good things and there had been nothing much he could do for Ruby. Nor much for himself but hard work and privation.

At that, Ruby had stuck by him even after he began to hit the bottle too hard. She used to talk of having a nice house somewhere, and maybe of traveling, seeing the world and meeting people. All he had given her was a series of small mining camps, ramshackle cabins, and nothing much to look forward to but more of the same. His dream, like so many others, was to make the big strike, but he never had.

The tinhorn was a slick talker and Ruby was pretty, prettier than most. He had talked mighty big of the places he would show her, and what they would do. Even when Dud followed him home one night and gave him a beating, Ruby had continued to meet him. Then they ran off.

At the time they had been just breaking even on what he made from odd jobs, and then he got a steady job with the stage line. He rushed home with the news, for it meant he'd have charge of the station at Haver Hill, a cool, pleasant little house where they could raise some chickens and have a flower garden as well as a place to raise garden truck. It was always given to a married man, and he had landed it. He rushed home with the news.

The house was empty. He had never seen it so empty because her clothes were gone and there was only the note . . . he still had it . . . telling him she was leaving him.

He gave up Haver Hill then and took a series of bad stations where the work was hard and there was much fighting. His salary wasn't bad and he had saved some money, bought a few horses, and broke teams during his spare time. The stage company itself had bought horses from him, and he was doing well. For the first time he managed to save some money, to get ahead.

There was no word from Ruby, although he never stopped hoping she would write. He did not want her back, but he hoped she was doing well and was happy. Also, he wanted her to know how well he was doing.

He did hear about the tinhorn, and it was from Brad Delaney that he got the news. The tinhorn had showed up in El Paso alone. From there he drifted north to Mobeetie, and finally to Fort Griffin. There he had tried to outsmart a man who was smarter, and when caught cheating he tried to outdraw him.

"What happened?" Dud had asked.

"What could happen? He tackled a man who wouldn't take anything from anybody, some fellow who used to be a dentist but was dying of tuberculosis. That dentist put two bullets into that tinhorn's skull, and he's buried in an unmarked grave in Boot Hill."

Dud Ryan wrote to El Paso, but the letter was returned. There was no trace of Ruby. Nobody knew where the tinhorn had come from and the trail ended there. Ryan had about convinced himself that Ruby was dead.

He tried to move, but the agony in his back held him still. If only he could live long enough! Where the hell was the stage? It should have been along hours ago.

He ground his teeth in pain and set his mind on the one thought: *Live! Live! Live!*

Delaney, Wells, and old Kickapoo were too good to die in an ambush. They were strong men, decent men, the kind the country needed. They wouldn't have let him down, and he'd be damned if he would fail them.

I'm tough, he told himself, I'm tough enough to last.

He tried, and after a moment succeeded in lifting his hand. His fingers were clumsy and his hand felt cold. There were no Indians in sight, but he dared not fire anyway, for he could never load the gun again. He just had to wait . . . somehow.

He could no longer make out the split logs in the ceiling. The shadows were darker now, and the room was darker. Was it really that much later? Or was he dying? Was this part of it?

Once he thought he heard a far-off yell, and he gripped the triggers of the shotgun, but the yell was not repeated. His lips fumbled for words, fumbled through the thickening fog in his brain. *Live!* he told himself. You've got to *live!*

"Ruby," he muttered, " 's all right, Ruby. I don't blame you."

He worked his mouth, but his lips were dry, and his tongue felt heavy in his mouth. "Live!" he whispered. "Please, God! Let me live!"

Something stirred in the brush across the way, and the shadow of movement caught his eye. An Indian was peering toward the station. And then wild and clear he heard Kickapoo's yell. "*Yeeow!*"

Dud Ryan felt a fierce surge of joy. He's made it! By the Lord Harry, he'd—! He tried to squeeze, but his fingers failed him and his hand fell away, fell to the floor.

He could hear the pound of hooves now, and the rattle of the stage.

He rolled over, the stabbing pain from his broken spine wrenching a scream from him, but in a last, terrible burst of energy he managed to grasp the rawhide in his teeth and jerk down. The twin barrels of the shotgun thundered, an enormous bellow of sound, in the empty room. Instantly there was a crash of sound, the rolling stage, rifles firing, and all hell breaking loose outside.

Kickapoo Jackson was rolling the stage down the slight hill to Bluff Creek when he heard the roar of the gun. Brad Delaney came up on his knees, rifle in hand, but it was Wells with the revolving shotgun who saw the first Indian. His shotgun bellowed and Delaney's rifle beat out a rapid tattoo of sound, and from below pistols and a rifle were firing.

The attack began and ended in that brief instant of gunfire, for the Indians were no fools and their ambush had failed. Swiftly, they retired, slipping away in the gathering darkness and carrying three dead warriors with them.

Jackson sawed the team to a halt, and Delaney dropped to the ground and sent three fast shots after the retreating Indians.

Doc Moody pushed open the door and saw the dying man, the rawhide still gripped in his teeth. With a gentle hand he took it away.

"You don't need to tell me, Doc. I've had it." Sweat beaded his forehead. "I've known for . . . hours. Had— had to . . . warn . . ."

Hank Wells dropped to his knees beside Ryan. "Dud, you saved us all, but you saved more than you know. You saved your own son!"

"Son?"

"Ruby had a boy, Dud. Your boy. He's four now, and he's outside there with Ma Harrigan."

"My boy? I saved my boy?"

"Ruby's dead, Ryan," Delaney said. "She was sending the boy to you, but we'll care for him, all of us."

He seemed to hear, tried to speak, and died there on the floor at Bluff Creek Station.

Doc Moody got to his feet. "By rights," he said, "that man should have been dead hours ago."

"Guts," Hank Wells said, "Dud never had much but he always had guts."

Doc Moody nodded. "I don't know how you boys feel about it, but I'm adopting a boy."

"He'll have four uncles then," Jackson said. "The boy will have to have a family."

"Count us in on that," the newlywed said. "We want to be something to him. Maybe a brother and sister, or something."

They've built a motel where the stage station stood, and not long ago a grandson and a great-grandson of Dud Ryan walked up the hill where some cedar grew, and stood beside Dud Ryan's grave. They stopped only a few minutes, en route to a family reunion.

There were fifty-nine descendants of Dud Ryan, although the name was different. One died in the Argonne Forest and two on a beach in Normandy, and another died in a hospital in Vietnam after surviving an ambush. There were eleven physicians and surgeons at the reunion, one ex-governor, two state senators, a locomotive engineer, and a crossing guard. There were two bus drivers and a schoolteacher, several housewives, and a country storekeeper. They had one thing in common: They all carried the blood of Ryan, who died at Bluff Creek Station on a late October evening.

A Fresh Start

∾◦∽

by Don Coldsmith

Don Coldsmith has made his reputation as an excellent Western writer on the strength of his Spanish Bit series, a historical re-creation of the introduction of the horse to the Native Americans by the Spanish. Now spanning more than thirty novels, the series is a high-water mark for historical fiction. A lifelong native of Kansas, he practices what he writes about, raising cattle and Appaloosa horses on his ranch. Before that he had a variety of careers, including serving as an artilleryman at Fort Sill, a grain inspector, and a family practice physician. He has also published three nonfiction books about horses, *Horsin' Around, Horsin' Around Again,* and *Still Horsin' Around,* all based on his syndicated newspaper column.

JACK BURNS LEANED against the dusty windowsill, half asleep, but stiff from inaction. The big coach rocked and bounced on its heavy leather springs, occasionally bumping harder when one of the wheels struck a rut or a stone in the dusty road.

Some of the passengers wore linen "dusters" to protect their clothing. A constant cloud of fine particles sprayed up like splashed water from beneath the hooves of the horses, mixing with that from the wheels. From a distance, the yellowish swirl would appear like a plume, trailing behind the coach, hanging in the still desert air.

Jack had no duster. Few possessions, actually. The clothes he wore, an extra shirt, and a jacket, wrapped in a blanket roll on his saddle in the rack on top of the vehicle. Better luggage, that of the more affluent passengers, was protected at least somewhat, in the closed "boot" at the rear of the coach.

He was bored, and his mind wandered. He was a bit discouraged. More than a bit, maybe. His life was going nowhere. It had really never gone much of anywhere. It had been a series of accidents, tragedies, and misfortunes. Here he was, past forty, traveling on a stage to nowhere. At least he estimated his age about there. No records were available. It seemed a reflection of his whole life.

He could barely remember his childhood. The mind tends to discard the unpleasant and savor the good things. But in his early years, there were virtually no good times. His earliest memories were of a warm, earth-bermed lodge in which his extended family lived. Possibly forty or fifty people, he'd been told, though that seemed unlikely to him. He'd had a mother and a father, whom he could hardly remember now. An uncle named Swimmer . . .

He still dreamed, sometimes, about The Fire, and would waken, wondering if he had screamed out loud. He thought of it as The Fire, though he realized now that it had been a genocidal raid by Delawares on his Pawnee village. He had been told that, when he was older. There had been few survivors. His mother had died defending her home. His father, a white man, had been absent. He had hated him for that.

The boy had been rescued from the burned rubble. By whom, he had no idea. He had been taken to an "Indian School," where he had been given a name . . . John, a good Christian name, and Burns, for the horrible scars down one side of his back and shoulder. It still itched sometimes when he was hot and sweaty, and the contraction of the scar somewhat limited his motion. It was a little better now, due to a sympathetic doctor. He had, with the help of considerable whiskey administered to both patient and physician, slashed the scar in three places to relieve the pull of the contracture. A blinding burst of pain, and a period of slow healing. But it was better. . . .

HE HAD BECOME disillusioned with the white man's mission school. They had tried to teach him to be ashamed of his heritage.

"You have to overcome it, John."

He was fortunate in one way. As a "breed," his skin was lighter than most. If he dressed the part and cut his hair short, he could easily pass for white. Especially if he allowed his beard to grow. It was a bit scraggly. His mustache was somewhat fuller. He had a mustache just now. It would never be the full, Dutchy mustache available to some, but it helped. He could pass for a suntanned paleface, maybe a little Mexican blood. The farther southwest, the easier that was accepted. Possibly that was why he had found himself on this stagecoach. Or maybe not. He wasn't certain that he had a reason. But everybody has to be somewhere, no?

He liked to be around horses. They ask fewer questions than people. He had apparently retained, from his Pawnee childhood, some of the native communication skills of his people. Communication with earth and sky and living things. His spirit meshed well with that of horses. It was a useful gift, one that found him in demand.

Probably, he estimated, he was still in his teens when he joined the Army. Not as a soldier. Not even as a scout. He could have been hired as a scout, except that he knew nothing about scouting. He was not eligible for an enlistment as a soldier, but the Army was hiring civilian teamsters, and he did know horses.

John had spent three years at that. There was no need to lie about his age. He didn't *know* his age, so he wasn't actually lying, he told himself. It was more of an exaggerated estimate.

There came a time when the Army was cutting back on civilian contracts, though, and he found himself searching.

Near a place called Kansas City, he found work at a livery stable, then as a handyman and sometimes a driver for a business called Sterling and Van Landingham. The company had varied assets. Overland shipping, both freight and passengers, and a fleet of riverboats on the Kaw and the Missouri Rivers.

One of the partners in the business, a gentleman named Jedediah Sterling, had taken an interest in him. There were special jobs, ones that indicated a trust on the part of the white man. Sterling actually seemed to have an understanding of the problems of an orphan half-breed, trying to find a place between two worlds.

Occasionally, John would be assigned jobs at the home of the Sterlings, such as splitting and stacking firewood. He met the wife of Mr. Sterling, a strikingly beautiful woman, somewhat younger than her husband. She too was good to him. Mrs. Sterling was almost as dark-skinned as John himself, and he wondered whether she might have Indian blood. Maybe that would explain the understanding of spirit that he thought he felt in Mr. Sterling.

Best of all, the chore-jobs at the Sterling house allowed him to be near their daughter, Neosho. She had been named, he was told, for the river that crosses the old Santa Fe Road at the Council Grove. They had lived there at the time the girl was born. Mr. Sterling had been a trapper, a "mountain man," and a scout for the Army in earlier days.

In the eyes of young John, Neosho was even more beautiful than her mother. She was perhaps a few years younger than he, and in the bloom of young womanhood. Better yet, Neosho seemed attracted to him. The two quickly became friends, and the girl's parents seemed not to object. He could not believe this good fortune. Maybe his luck was changing at last.

Things had progressed to the point where the inevitable conversation must take place. That of a father's questions to his prospective son-in-law. Even that had seemed to go well for a while. Then, for reasons he had not understood, an anxious look had crept over Sterling's face as he continued his questioning about the massacre and The Fire. John began to realize that he had very little knowledge of his family.

The questions continued.

"Your mother is dead, John?"

"Yes, sir. She was killed fighting the Delawares. My older sister was killed too, in the fire."

Mr. Sterling seemed to be increasingly concerned, far beyond that which could be expected. His voice was husky.

"What . . . What was your uncle's name, John?"

"Swimmer. My mother's brother. Why?"

Sterling was silent, his face pale.

"What is it?" John asked.

"John, I have to tell you. You cannot court Neosho."

It hurt all the more, coming from a man he respected. John stood and rose to his full height, his pride offended.

"Because I am Pawnee, or just because I am a savage? I would not have thought this from *you*, Mr. Sterling."

"No, no, that is not it, John."

"Then *what*?"

"My heart is very heavy with this, my son," Sterling said slowly. Somehow John felt that it sounded like listening to an elder of his own people. "It is not easy. Your mother was Raven, no?"

"I had not told you that."

"I know. Your sister's name was Cherry Flower, and your own, Little Elk."

"How do you know these things?"

"My name was Long Walker."

"*You?* You are my *father*?"

A wave of confusion washed over him, which quickly turned to rage.

"You *left* us!" he accused.

"It was not like that," Sterling protested. "I was away. John, I loved your mother very much. I love her memory still. The town was dead when I returned. *Gone,* all of our People. I was told that *you* were dead."

Now John was flooded with a mix of emotion. He had found his father, and the mystery of abandonment was solved. That was good to have learned.

But the other . . .

"Then," he said slowly, hopelessly, "Neosho is . . ."

"Yes . . ." Sterling nearly choked on the words. "You can't court her. She is your sister."

IT HAD BEEN an insufferable mix of emotions, on that day long ago. All his life, he had wondered about his father. Hated him for abandoning his family. He had dreamed of tracking the man down and killing him. He would do it slowly, painfully, in some exotic way. Torture . . .

Now, he had found the man, after all these years. It was almost a disappointment to find that he liked and respected the father whom he had presumed to hate. And his father was a man who respected and understood the Indian people, and those of mixed blood. It had been *his* way.

But what should have been a triumphant and joyous reunion was spoiled. Destroyed, in fact, by the tragic circumstances of a love that could never be.

It had taken him only a few hours to realize that it was an impossible situation. He could not become a part of this comfortable and loyal family; could not see the girl he loved marry another man and bear *his* children.

Knowing the Sterlings as he now felt he did, he was certain that his father would try to do something for a long-lost son. Set him up in business or in ranching somewhere, out of contact with Neosho. But John knew it would never work. It would only be a hurt to all parties involved. No, it would be better to sever all ties quickly. It would be painful, but in the long run, better for all.

There was a horse at the livery where he had been living that he had talked of buying. The livery man also owed him money, for some horse-breaking that he'd been doing on the side. More than the horse was worth.

He thought of telling Sterling, or leaving a note, but decided against it. He'd rather not leave a trail. Late that night he quietly rolled his blankets, saddled the gelding, and departed. He doubted that his father would try to find him. He was also certain that Sterling would understand, and probably approve. Probably share the tragic secret with Mrs. Sterling, but not with their daughter.

Neosho would be heartbroken, would not understand, would probably come to hate him. That was just as well. Better that she should hate than that she should live with a heartbreak such as he felt. She would find someone else. Someone that he hoped would be worthy of her. He had fantasies of returning to see that she was properly treated and respected.

THE SWAYING AND bumping of the coach jarred him back to reality. It was hot and dusty, crowded and uncomfortable. Maybe he should have offered to sit up with the driver. Maybe he'd offer to do so at the next stop.

He looked at each of the other passengers in turn, some sleepy, some uncomfortable. Some appeared almost happy, despite the uncomfortable circumstances. He wondered about their stories. They'd never understand his, but some might have back trails as gnarled and twisted as his own.

AFTER HE LEFT Kansas City, he had moved from one place to another. Small towns, ranches . . . odd jobs for a

meal or two, a place to sleep in the barn. He'd earn a few
dollars and move on, restless and unsettled. He had not
quite realized that he was trying to run from a past that
was unshakable. It clung to him like a cocklebur that he
couldn't reach, and chafed him at every move.

He had been down on his luck in New Orleans when
he took a job as a stevedore, loading a ship bound for
South America. When the ship's officer offered him pas-
sage to help with the unloading at the other end, he accepted.

"Can't get good help down there," the man explained.

He knew enough Spanish to get by, and understood
more than he could speak. It was good to feel solid ground
under his feet at Buenos Aires, and he'd decided to stay
a little while. Not in the city, but in open grazing country
like that which he knew.

He felt at home with horses and cattle and *vaqueros.*
The Argentinian cowboys used a *bola,* quite different
from the lariats with which he was familiar. It was a three-
part braided affair, ends tied together in the middle, and
with a rock the size of an apple at each outer end. He
never mastered the use of the *bola,* and marveled that no
animal ever seemed to be injured by the whirling missiles.

Fortunately, horses spoke the same tongue everywhere,
and he was successful on the pampas as well as the prairie
when it came to taming and breaking to saddle.

AFTER A SEASON or two he realized that he could run but
not hide, and worked his way back to the States as he had
come. He drifted, town to town. There was a space that
he didn't even remember, when he was drinking heavily,
gambling, and trying to escape into a different existence.

That phase ended when he awoke in a muddy gutter
one morning, without the slightest idea how he got there,
and unable to recall the name of the town. His pockets
were empty. It took a little while to recall that he had

been talking and drinking with a painted woman at a bar. She had urged him to have "one more for the road." He realized now that it had probably been drugged.

There had been other women, through the years. Some better than others, in various ways. He had left behind a *señorita* in Argentina, who had tried to read more into their relationship than he felt. He was sure that she had felt abandoned. Probably she had cried, and for that his heart was heavy. But it was a mistake on her part. Another mistake would not have corrected the first.

Some of the women he had been with were actually unattractive, now that he looked back. Dim light, loneliness, and liquor do much to enhance the attractiveness of the opposite sex. On occasion, he had found himself embarrassed and repulsed later, in the stark reality of day.

Gradually, he had come to accept that romance was not to be his. Each relationship in turn reinforced this theory, and he began to avoid contacts that might have any potential for meaning. Stated bluntly, he had come to avoid women. Especially decent women. There were few on the frontier anyway.

Soon, any relationship became merely one to satisfy need. It was like eating, in a way. One eats for subsistence. For survival. One eats what is available, for better or worse, and sometimes refrains when the available fare is of questionable quality. Sometimes it is preferable to go hungry. And fasting is respectable.

HE SPENT SOME time in Mexico, but it was no better than Argentina. On his return, he continued to wander. California, Oregon, Utah, Dakota. He avoided the center of the country, his original home, because he did not want to risk contact with the Sterlings. That could bring nothing but hurt.

Even thinking about them brought hurt. He had been able to realize and accept that his father was not to blame. He did not feel that he must forgive, because there was

nothing to forgive. It had been a part of the tragedy. His
father could not have known.

More difficult was his love for Neosho. He still
dreamed of her sometimes, though not as often now. He
could remember her smile, the shape of her lithe young
body, and sway of her hips as she walked. He had found
her so desirable, so beautiful. It was still impossible to
see her in any other way. Certainly not as his sister.

He often wondered where she was now. With a pain
in his heart, he wondered who now shared her bed. Then
the guilt over such thoughts made his heart heavy. He
tried his best to avoid them.

AS HE WANDERED, running from his past, he had done a
variety of work. Mostly with horses. Somewhere along
the line, while working on a ranch, he had changed his
name. There were too many men named John. The
rancher himself was John Jones, sometimes called J.J.
This was reflected in the JJ brand. The cook was John
too. Still another John was called Preacher, because he
had an affinity for reading his Bible in the bunkhouse.
Preacher good-naturedly called attention to the scriptural
reference and suggested that they could be First John, Second John, and Third John, as in the books of the Bible.
This brought a guffaw of laughter, but little acceptance.

In the end, there were J.J., Cookie, Preacher, and John
Burns, who soon became "Burns." The only one actually
called John was the foreman, John Evans. It was he who
probably guessed the origin of Burns's name. With feeling
for the scars, both physical and emotional, he suggested
that the newcomer be titled "Jack," a common synonym
for John.

John Burns rather liked it, and used it after he left the
JJ. It might help to remove himself from the tragedy of
his past. He might be more difficult to trace if any of the
Sterlings attempted to locate him. He did not think they

would want to do so, but . . . anyway, it might help him to distance himself from the heartbreak.

This, of course, was unsuccessful, but he kept the name anyway. *Jack* Burns . . .

THE COACH BOUNCED and wakened him again. He had dozed off in his reverie without realizing. He was slightly embarrassed, and looked around him at the other passengers. The man beside him had also fallen asleep, and had sagged over toward Jack, almost leaning against him. Their eyes met for a moment.

"Sorry," the man mumbled.

Jack nodded, and the two looked elsewhere, in opposite directions.

A woman on the other seat, facing them, was adjusting her hat. It had apparently been knocked askew by the same jolt that had wakened him.

He took a deep breath and retreated again into his memory.

THE CLOSEST HE had ever come to a vocation, other than odd jobs, was, like everything else in his life, an accident. He had been down on his luck for the hundredth time, out of money and with no prospects.

He had not even had the few coins it might have taken to get into a poker game. He had done that before, though he didn't like the game. He often found that he was able to read the faces of the other players. Consequently he could bet, call, or drop out at the proper time. He was so successful at it, in fact, that he had been accused of cheating. There had been a narrow escape or two, as he was searched for hidden cards in his sleeve or in his boot tops.

No, gambling was too dangerous anyway. There were too many who would accuse, and shoot first, even before they asked questions. Before the accused had a chance to prove his innocence.

Besides, he felt guilty when he gambled, as if he *were* taking unfair advantage of the situation. His uncle Swimmer had called it a gift, this ability to see things that others do not.

"You must not misuse this gift," his uncle had emphasized. "To use it selfishly or to hurt others will turn the spirits *against* you, and destroy your gift."

"Then, I would be no different from anyone else?" the boy had asked.

"Worse maybe," Swimmer had answered. "If you use it to hurt others, it could kill you."

So, he avoided gambling when he could.

ON THE OCCASION in question, however, he did not even have a stake. He had ridden into a dusty little town in Colorado. He watered his horse at the public trough, to give him a chance to look around.

A group of men were standing near a corral at the livery stable, obviously talking about a horse. It was, also obviously, not a private discussion. He sauntered over to see what was going on.

The horse in question was a bald-faced blue roan, standing sleepily in the sun, hip-shot with one back foot resting on the tip of the hoof. There was something about the horse that made Jack think that this appearance was deceptive. One man, obviously the owner, was doing the talking.

". . . an' he's damn near killed a couple of men," the man went on. "It ain't that he's mean. Plumb gentle to handle. Jest likes to buck. An' he don't hold no grudges. No comin' after you with hoofs an' teeth once you're off, like some ol' killer'll do. Once he's won, the game's over, no hard feelin's."

"And he ain't never been rode?" asked one of the cowboys.

"No, siree! You stay on him to the count of ten, you

win. Costs you ten dollars to try, an' you get a hunnerd if you stay on."

Jack Burns had been studying the horse. The roan was calm and self-assured, confident. A man would have to earn that confidence to handle such a horse. He leaned against the fence, then reached across the top rail to touch the proud neck, damp from the sweat of the hot, sunny day. He removed his hat with his left hand and wiped his own sweaty brow with the fingers of his right. Then he reached to pat the horse again, mixing the scent of the two. Their medicines.

It had been long ago when as a boy he had seen this maneuver carried out by his uncle, Swimmer, when taming a horse. "It shows him *'our medicines mix well, with no harm to either,'*" Swimmer had explained.

It was not long after that when the tragedy struck the town, and everything was lost. Even, for a while, the memory of that lesson. Young Little Elk had not had the opportunity to try it, and in fact had forgotten it until this moment.

Now Jack Burns stroked the soft silken skin around the nostrils with those same fingers, while the roan sniffed curiously.

"I'll try him," he said, "but I haven't got your ten dollars."

"Sorry, boy," said the promoter. "No bets without somethin' to back 'em up. What you got?"

"Nothin' much, or I wouldn't be tryin' this, would I?" The crowd chuckled.

"Then don't waste my time," the horse owner warned. "I'm here to do business. Anybody else want to fork the Widow Maker here?"

There was another quiet chuckle, but no one seemed anxious to call attention to himself with any kind of remark. There were certainly no challengers.

Jack spoke again.

"I'd bet my saddle."

The horse owner glanced over at Jack's dun, standing at the hitch rail.

"That one?"

"Yes, sir."

"Hell, I don't need a saddle," he snorted. "But I'll take a look."

He shuffled through the dust and looked over the well-used saddle, lifting the saddle roll behind the cantle to see whether there was any damage. He tugged at the horn. It was a well-worn but soiled hull, showing honest use, and well worth forty or fifty dollars.

"Well, it ain't much," he said with a touch of contempt. "But mebbe I can sell it. Okay, let's go!"

Excitement mounted as the roan was prepared for the contest. The animal's calm attitude changed, and he began to fidget, dancing a little as they drew the cinch tight.

Jack stood at the horse's head, rubbing the nose and crooning softly in his ear. The horse steadied. The owner brought a blindfold, and wrapped it around the head. Jack blew gently in the ear, and gave one last stroke to the nose, then stepped into the stirrup and lifted his right leg over the saddle, settling in and finding the other stirrup.

"Where's your spurs?" asked the owner.

"Don't use 'em," said Jack.

"You got to spur him!" insisted the other. "Make him buck."

"You didn't say nothin' about spurrin' him. You said *ride* him."

"That's right," said one of the onlookers. "You didn't say *spur* him out."

The owner was still holding the horse's blindfold. His face was tense and angry. This was not going well. But he had to make a move. He whipped the towel away from the horse's face, letting the bright sunlight suddenly strike the eyes. At the same moment, he jabbed a thumb into the roan's soft flank.

The roan erupted in a mighty leap, and Jack clung to

the halter rope and the saddle horn. Three long, stiff-legged jumps, each jarring the rider to the very marrow of his bones.

The owner was counting aloud, barely heard over the yells of the spectators.

". . . four . . . five . . ."

The count was very slow. It was quickly apparent that the promoter knew he was in trouble, and wanted to prolong the ride until the horse could dislodge the rider.

". . . six . . . seven . . ."

The crowd was counting aloud now, pulling for the rider, forcing a legitimate count. Another halfhearted buck or two, and the roan began to run instead of bucking. He circled the corral at a fast lope, around and around, the rider still clinging tightly, and the crowd cheering.

". . . eight . . . nine . . . *ten!*"

Another circuit or two, and the horse slowed. Jack pulled on the halter-shank and the animal stopped before the crowd, hardly breathing more heavily than normal.

"I'll try him!" yelled a cowboy.

"I'm next!" laughed another. "Here's my ten!"

"No!" stated the promoter firmly. "No more today. He's sick, or somebody's drugged him."

His face was livid as the crowd began to disperse, still laughing.

Jack stepped down, brushing dust from his shirt and jeans. He patted the horse again.

Grudgingly, the promoter counted out five twenty-dollar gold pieces. His anger was cooling somewhat.

"You got me good, boy. I'm through in this town. But there's another'n, down the road."

Jack pocketed the money. It would provide the start he needed.

Now, his temper abating, the promoter seemed to carry no grudge.

"Lemme ask you," he said, "what the hell did you *do*? I musta missed it."

Jack smiled thinly. "Just an ol' Indian trick or two."

"I figgered as much. You're good with a horse, boy. But can I give you some advice?"

"Reckon so."

"Okay. I figger you to be a real rider. Not many could have stayed on with the three jumps ol' Roanie started out with. But you got sumpin' to learn: Never bet your saddle."

"What do you mean?"

"You bet me your saddle, and you mighta lost it."

"But I didn't."

"I know. But you *might* have. Now, a rider like you can always make it, breakin' horses or bettin' on whether you can ride an outlaw critter. But you need your saddle. Bet your boots or your hat, even your horse, but if you still got your saddle you can get a fresh start."

"Sounds like you've been there."

"I have, boy. You remind me of myself about thirty years ago, before the war. You can travel an' offer to ride horses that can't be rode. Every town, every ranch, has one, almost. You make your money not from *breakin'* horses, but from bettin' on whether you can or not. You win some, lose some, but win a lot more'n you lose. And as long as you got your saddle, you can start over."

THAT HAD LED to a new phase of his life. Jack had traveled, handled horses, ridden outlaw broncs, and had made a good living betting on the outcome. He was grateful to the nameless promoter who had given him sound advice years before.

As he expected, he won some and lost some. Occasionally he was sidelined by injuries. A broken arm, an ankle, a couple of ribs . . . Once, an ear torn nearly off when a bronc that had thrown him stepped on his head. It had healed better than he expected.

*   *   *

BUT NOW, HE had the feeling that time was running out. He was suddenly old. He didn't know when it had happened. And he wasn't really old, he told himself. Not like the doddering old men he saw on benches in front of the storefronts in towns all across the frontier. He, Jack Burns, couldn't be much more than forty. But there was the ache and stiffness that he felt on frosty mornings. The little bit of extra effort it now took to step up into the saddle of a tall horse. The aches that foretold a change in the weather. He used to chuckle at the old men who talked of such things. Now, it was no laughing matter.

On the day he was dumped, hard, by a horse that should have been easy, he realized that it was over. He couldn't continue going down road after road, risking his neck riding outlaw broncs. He'd have to find something else. But first, he needed a rest. He'd head for a warmer climate that might be more friendly for his aching bones. Maybe Arizona.

He had very little money to tide him over. Maybe he could become a horse trader. If there was anything he did know about, it was horses.

THE COACH RATTLED and rumbled on. He felt dejected. He really had no plan as to what he'd do once they arrived at their destination.

Tombstone. Odd name for a town. He'd seen towns all over the West. A lot of them had strange names. Sleepily, he thought about that for a while, his mind wandering idly. A lot of towns were named for people. One of the founders maybe. The town would preserve that name long after that person was dead and gone.

A lot of it was political. Towns all over the border states were named to show the sympathies of the inhabitants in the recent War Between the States. Union City . . . Some places had even *changed* their names to reflect their loyalties. There were several called Independence or Liberty.

On the other hand, there were places with names that reflected earlier inhabitants' presence. Many had outlived occupation by a succession of claimants . . . Spanish, French, Mexican, the Republic of Texas, the Confederate States, and the United States. Some with French or Spanish names were based on a physical description or an event that had occurred there. Often the physical description transcended the language and the culture. Big Bend, Grand Island, Council Grove . . .

Sometimes people named their new homes for the place they came from, with or without a "New" designation. New York, New England, New Jersey . . .

His favorite names described the spirit of a place, or its effect on the inhabitants. Pretty Prairie, Pleasant Ridge, Pleasanton, Green Valley, Warm Springs, Climax . . . Even such desperate designations as Hope.

Sometimes a place would be named to commemorate a bad or unfortunate situation. Troublesome Creek, Dead Horse, Starving Woman Creek, Last Chance . . .

HE SIGHED AND shifted his position to relieve the stiffness in his muscles. He'd be glad to reach Tombstone, though he had little idea what he'd do when he arrived. Actually, he wondered why he'd decided to go there anyway.

He was down and out again. He'd lost his horse in a bet, gotten thrown by a bronc he should have handled easily. Could have, a few years ago. But his reflexes were slowing. That fraction of a heartbeat that it took him to read the intention of the powerful creature beneath him had become longer now.

And now, he was just about at the end of his rope. He still had his saddle, but it no longer had the potential for earning a new start that it had once possessed. No, that wasn't quite right, he thought wryly. *The saddle still has it, but the rider doesn't.*

Maybe it was appropriate that the wheels on the big

coach were whirling toward a place called Tombstone. He
hadn't thought of that. He only knew that in some strange
way, he belonged here on this coach. He was meant to
make this journey, no matter how it was to end.

There were some things about his Pawnee heritage that
the white government schools had not managed to wring
out of him. One was the deep-seated faith in dreams or
visions. Such a gift was not to be ignored, even if it made
no sense at the time. Therefore, when he woke in the
hayloft at the livery, stiff and sore from the beating he
had taken from the black mustang, he knew. In his dream,
or vision (or are they not much the same anyway?), he
had been climbing into a big red stagecoach.

He had seldom traveled that way. Usually, it was from
town to town, on his own horse. He had lost that now.
He did have a couple of gold pieces, by means of which
he had boarded the stage. He'd had to ask where it was
going. Tombstone. Why? He had no idea, but he was
certain that it was right. Had he not seen this in the
dream?

Maybe this Tombstone would be a place where he
could make a new start in a new way. He did have some
skills besides riding broncs. He was good at repairing a
saddle or bridle or harness. That had been a necessity.
Maybe he could work for a harness maker or saddler.

He could still use the spirit-skills that had been handed
to him with his heritage. His ability to communicate with
horses. Maybe he'd tried too hard to mix the different
methods. The "breaking" of the horse, as compared to
mingling with its spirit.

He did know horses, and knew them well. In the past
few years he had seen many professional horse traders.
He had seen every trick and deception that could be imagined. He could not exactly visualize himself using some
of these questionable practices. Could there be such a
thing as an honest horse trader? he asked himself with
wry humor.

Well, what will be, will be. . . .

*   *   *

WHEN HE STEPPED down from the stage in Tombstone, he had no idea what to expect. He helped the driver retrieve his saddle and blanket roll, and wandered over to the boardwalk in front of one of the saloons. The smell of stale smoke and liquor drifted from the doorway, and he thought about going in. He quickly decided against it. He had, at one time, traveled too far down that road, and knew its dangers.

Instead, he decided to orient himself with a livery stable. Most liveries would allow him to sleep in their loft, and he could make himself useful while he waited to see what happened next.

Tombstone was a lot bigger than he'd imagined. There was a hustle and bustle that one might expect in a prosperous mining town. It had grown in less than a decade, he quickly learned, from a silver camp, named as a joke. ("You're more likely to find your tombstone than your fortune!")

He'd been in some mining towns before, and in some respects they were all alike.

Jack had never been able to understand the mentality of such a town. Everyone seems to feel immortal, and on the verge of a great revelation that will mean wealth, without any work or effort. There is an air of adolescent excitement, a giddy, careless expectancy that assumes that everyone will be a winner. Here too there was the disproportion of businesses found in such a town. Far more saloons and bawdy houses and gambling places than schools and churches. Stores were stocked unpredictably with goods in demand, whether necessities or whimsical desires, and all at inflated prices.

It recalled to him a part of a winter he'd spent in San Francisco. An acquaintance, equally down on his luck, continually referred to how wonderful everything would be "when my ship comes in." Jack, at last tired of the poor excuse for clever banter, finally put it to rest:

"Bill, did you ever send one *out*?"

Tombstone seemed much like that to him. Thousands of people, scurrying like ants but with much less organization, hurrying to nowhere to do nothing constructive.

He was a bit puzzled as to how he came to be here, but did not question it. He was here, now. So be it. There was no way to leave until he could find a way to earn enough money to pay his way out. Or, of course, to buy a horse and enough provisions to ride out. The fastest way would have been to bet on his skill at riding somebody's bronc. He'd done that, many times. But that had been when his body was younger. His mind told him that at forty-something he was still a young man in his prime. His bones and muscles slyly suggested a somewhat different interpretation. Especially considering the way these same bones and muscles had been abused. No, he'd not do that. It was too risky. It was chilling to think that he might be not only penniless but crippled if the ride did not go well.

HE FOUND A small livery stable on the outskirts of town, and offered to clean stalls in exchange for a place to sleep.

The proprietor looked him over, noting the well-used saddle and neatly packed roll.

"Just get to town?"

Jack nodded.

"Where's your hoss?"

"Don't have one. Came on the stage."

The liveryman nodded. He could read a lot by what he saw. A pretty good horseman, down on his luck . . .

"Okay. You can sleep in the tack room. There's a cot. Kid I had ran off to git rich. Ain't goin' to, likely."

Jack merely nodded.

HE SHOOK OUT the grimy blankets on the cot in the tack room, hung them outside to sun, and then decided to use his own. He'd wash the others later. But just now he'd have to earn his keep.

It was quickly apparent why the liveryman was so willing to furnish him a place to sleep. The stalls were in bad shape. Only a few were relatively clean and with fresh bedding straw. Some toward the back were deep in soiled bedding. Jack forked barrow after barrow of manure and wet straw, and trundled it to the manure pile out behind the stable.

Evening fell before he had fairly started, but his work had made some notable progress. The liveryman glanced in shortly before sunset, and said nothing. The man's whole attitude as he looked around, however, indicated his approval. About the time that Jack was washing up at the horse trough in front of the stable, the proprietor returned. He was carrying a tin plate with a half-dozen biscuits and a few thick strips of fried salt pork.

"The missus thought mebbe you could use some supper," he said.

"Sure can! Thank you."

The biscuits were light and flaky, the mark of a good cook. The salt pork was salt pork, but nothing much was to be expected. In the gift, though, was an unspoken statement of appreciation and mutual understanding that said much more.

Jack sought his bed, tired and stiff, but looking forward to the sleep that is the reward of honest labor.

HE WOKE SOME time later to answer the call of his full bladder. He had no watch, but the moon was rising, a few nights past full. Must be about midnight. It was light enough to find his way out toward the manure pile. No point in using the outhouse merely to satisfy his present need.

He was just rebuttoning his jeans when he noticed some restlessness among the horses in a little corral to the north of the main pens. Something going on? Keeping in the shadow of the big barn, he slipped toward the source of the unrest.

There was enough moonlight to see fairly well. A half-dozen animals circled the corral restlessly as a big man moved quietly among them. Jack stood very still, unsure of himself. What could possibly be a reason for anyone to be in the corral at this hour, with no light? It could not likely be any honest activity. Very quietly, he watched, nervously wishing he hadn't stumbled into whatever this was.

The man seemed to be concentrating on one particular horse, a big bay that Jack had noticed earlier. It was a far better animal than any others in the pen, and as such, had caught his eye. This pen of horses, he'd been told, was to be auctioned the next morning. Was the big man trying to affect that sale in some way?

Now he had tossed a soft cotton rope across the neck of the bay and slipped a loop around its nose. The well-trained gelding stood unexcited, as the man ran expert hands over its back and rump. He stopped at the tail, combing out the long hair with his fingers. He took something from his pocket, small knife probably, and appeared to cut a few strands of horsehair. Then he returned to the front of the animal and picked up to the foot.

Jack held his breath. He wished that he hadn't seen this. He had a pretty good idea, now, of the skullduggery in progress. It took only a short while. The knife came out again for a last quick purpose, to trim the ends. The big man set the hoof back down, coiled his rope, and departed quickly, fading into the shadows.

Jack waited for several minutes to make certain the man was gone. He really wanted no part of this, but felt that he had need to verify what he'd seen. He slipped quietly into the corral and moved among the horses. His familiar scent did not disturb them as they munched hay from the rack.

He easily located the bay, half a hand taller than any of the others. He stroked the neck and shoulder and picked up the left front foot. His skilled fingers palpated the ankle. Yes, there it was. A slender strand of twisted horsehair from the tail, knotted tightly around the pastern just under the fetlock. By sale time tomorrow, the swelling would have begun. The horse would limp badly, and would appear to be unsound. This would effectively kill the bidding, and the perpetrator would buy the horse for a tiny fraction of its real value. When the sale was over, it required only to cut the horsehair circlet, and the animal was sound again.

It was a dastardly trick, one Jack had seen used before. Now he wished, more than ever, that he hadn't seen the act. What should he do? What *could* he do? Tell someone? He thought of confiding to the liveryman what he'd seen, but rejected that idea. Maybe it was part of *his* business. He hoped not.

He started back toward his bed, knowing he couldn't sleep. Almost there, he turned back. Win or lose, he had to do something. He took a quick look around from the vantage point of the barn's shadow, and then slipped into the pen again. He picked up the gelding's foot and took out his own pocketknife. A quick clip . . . He put the twist of horsehair in his pocket. He did not want anyone to find it and see that it had been cut. Quietly, he slipped back to the tack room and to a restless sleep until morning.

THE AUCTION WAS to start at noon, and a dozen prospective bidders were milling around the livery by mid-morning. Jack worked hard at his cleaning, fully intending to watch the sale. It should be interesting. He looked for a tall, big-shouldered man whom he might have seen before, but didn't spot him.

At about an hour before noon, a buggy drew up, carrying a man, a woman, and a boy of twelve or thirteen. The man jerked the team to a halt with a heavy hand, stepped down, and helped the woman to dismount. Then he lifted a hitching weight to the ground and snapped its strap into the bridle of the near horse. His movements seemed familiar. Could it be . . . ?

"Who's the folks in the buggy?" he asked a loiterer near him.

The man chuckled. "That's the Widow Moore. Her horses are sellin' today. That's her boy too."

"Who's the fella? A relative?"

"Not hardly! New fella in town. Name of Smith."

"Lots of fellas named Smith," observed another loiterer.

"Well, this one's been courtin' Miz Moore since he got here, couple o' months ago."

"She's a nice-looking woman," Jack observed.

It was a gross understatement, he knew full well. Here was a woman of character, one with pride and dignity. She reminded him of Mrs. Sterling, back so many years ago. About the same age that the mother of Neosho had been then, he figured. Mid to late thirties. She carried herself well, and with a confidence that he admired in a woman.

It distressed him that he was fairly certain the man with her was the man who had doctored the horse. If so, he was up to no good, in more ways than one.

Again, what could Jack do? it was really none of his business, but his basic integrity cried out against anyone who would take advantage of a woman, especially one in trouble. With his anger rising, he watched "Smith" step to the corral fence, appearing to evaluate the horses as they moved.

Jack saw a movement at his elbow, and glanced down. The Moore boy had slipped into an empty space, and was looking at the horses.

"That your daddy, boy?" Jack asked.

It was a stupid thing to say, but he felt a need to make a contact of some sort.

The boy looked up, a bit of resentment in his eyes.

"Not by a damn sight, mister."

"Hey, your mama wouldn't like you usin' those words."

"You know her?"

"Nope. But I can see she's a lady."

"You got that right! Too good for that four-flusher." The boy pointed to Smith.

"What's the matter with him?"

"Everything. I don't like the way he's sniffin' after my mama. I don't like the way he handles a horse. My daddy was a *horseman*. But why should I be talkin' to you?"

"I dunno. But I hear you. I lost my daddy too. I was younger'n you."

The boy looked at him with renewed interest.

"My name's Jack Burns," he said, extending his hand.

The boy took it. A confident, firm grip for a youngster. That was good. This boy would need it.

"Dave . . . David Moore. Named for my daddy."

"When did you lose him?"

" 'Bout a year ago."

"Accident?"

"Nope. A sickness. Typhoid or somethin', I guess. They wouldn't let me see him."

"That's too bad. But you know—"

"Yeah, I know why."

Now the auctioneer stepped up on a box and prepared to open the bidding.

"These here"—he pointed to the horses—"are part of the Dave Moore herd. We all know the kind of quality Dave's horses carry. Now, Mrs. Moore needs to sell off a few at a time here, while she decides how she's goin' to handle the estate of her late husband."

He went on, describing this lot, pointing out some of

the breeding. Some Arab blood, crossed with Morgan and a touch of Thoroughbred.

Now in daylight, Jack was more impressed with the quality of this group of animals. Still, the bay gelding was far above the others, and appeared to have a reputation for quality.

"Now, what am I bid for this dun filly?" the auctioneer began. "Three-year-old, green-broke, presumed open . . ."

It took a few moments to get the first bid. Jack was not surprised when it came from Mr. Smith.

"Fifty!"

"All right! Thankee, Mr. Smith. I have fifty, do I hear sixty-sixty-sixty-got it over there-sixty-hear seventy . . ."

The chant flowed on, mesmerizing the crowd. Smith continued to toss in a bid occasionally, and then dropped out as the contest narrowed to two other bidders. The technique was plain to Jack Burns. Smith would bid on each animal, establishing himself as a serious buyer, but not really buying. He was after the bay, which he expected to sell low on account of a contrived suspicion of unsoundness. A horse trader, a shrewd and dishonest one. Jack's anger rose again at the thought that such a man would prey on a woman's misfortune. It bothered him even more that the man was also trying to court such a woman in her bereavement. Jack was having a great deal of trouble convincing himself that all of this was none of his business.

"Going once . . . Twice . . . *Sold!*"

The auctioneer brought down his gavel with a hollow thump on the end of the keg he was using for a podium.

"To Mr. Jackson, there . . . Two-seventy-five! Now, let's look at the roan here."

A helper led the next animal around the ring, at a walk and trot as he had the dun, while the auctioneer requested the first bid. The process was much the same.

Jack found himself wishing that he had the money at hand to enter the bidding. These were good horses, and he needed one badly. But he still didn't even know what he was doing in Tombstone trying to get back on his feet.

Finally, the bay was led into the ring. Walk, trot, a short lope . . .

"What am I bid? Somebody start it. One of the best horses you'll see this year! Good bloodlines . . ."

The first bid was a hundred, and the auctioneer made a quick inquiry as to the man's connection with a glue factory. The crowd chuckled, relaxed and absorbed in the proceedings.

At two hundred, Smith stepped forward.

"Wait a moment, Colonel! I think the horse is limping. We don't want to mislead anyone as to his soundness."

Jack was offended at the man's presumption, and at the use of "we." Or was this courtship much farther along that he realized?

"All right, let's look at him," agreed the auctioneer. "I didn't see a limp, but we want an honest sale."

Smith stepped into the ring and approached the horse. Now, since the scheme had failed, the man was in a dilemma. Someone was going to check the horse's feet, and Mr. Smith needed to be the one.

He picked up the left front foot, examined the hoof, picked at the sole with his pocketknife, and seemed puzzled as he palpated the pastern and fetlock.

He has a right to be puzzled, thought Jack. Maybe worried just a little bit. Jack smiled to himself.

"We'll start the bidding over," announced the auctioneer.

He had a hard time getting the first bid, which was only thirty-five dollars.

"Stop!" called a woman's voice.

The crowd murmured and then was quiet.

Mrs. Moore walked up to the auctioneer.

"The horse is not for sale!" she announced. "There's something wrong here. I don't know what, but I'll find out!"

"Now, Amanda," said Mr. Smith, hurrying to her side. "Calm down. I'm here for you."

She whirled on him, furious.

"You!" she snapped. "You know there's nothing wrong with that horse! *You're* part of this. I don't know what you're up to, but I want you out of here, out of my life. I just wish I had the proof I need to show you up for what you are!"

A few feet away, Jack Burns stood, with an expressionless face. Inside, he was smiling. Now maybe he had some clue as to how he'd happened to land in Tombstone.

Beside him, Davey Moore was smiling.

"Boy, Mama told him, didn't she?" he said to Jack.

"She sure did, son."

Jack smiled too. He put a hand into the pocket of his jeans, and for reassurance, touched the slender strands of twisted horsehair. Maybe he was going to like Tombstone.

Hearts

❧

by Richard S. Wheeler

Richard Wheeler's highly detailed, deftly told Western novels have gained him a reputation for writing stories about ordinary people of the West and how their everyday lives can be just as enthralling as a gunslinger's or a desperado's. His third novel, *Winter Grass,* broke almost every convention of the traditional Western, and still received rave reviews and a nomination for the Western Writers of America's Spur Award for Best Novel. Wheeler used the skills he developed as a reporter for the *Oakland Tribune* in California and later as a staff writer for *Reader's Digest* and as a reporter, copy editor, and city editor for the *Billings Gazette* in Montana in his fiction writing. A winner of the Spur Award in 1989, he lives in Livingston, Montana.

LAURA DUVALL HAD expected every man in Tombstone to wear a side arm, but that was not what she discovered as the Wells Fargo agent opened the door of her coach. She did not see a holstered weapon. At least not at first.

She had choked on the golden dust all the way from Benson, along with the fumes emanating from seven overheated males jammed onto the sticky leather seats. She knew the Arizona heat would torment her, and had prepared for it as best she could with a dress of white muslin that filtered air through her gauzy camisole and petticoat.

It was her turn to step out, and as she did so she spotted
a familiar face in the shadow of the awning over the
boardwalk. John Behan, sheriff in Tombstone. She knew
him, but he didn't know her. She would have known him ·
even without the polished steel circlet on his chest. She
had studied numerous tintypes of him and had read
lengthy reports describing him. One thing he always did
was meet the stage.

And now he was lounging casually in the shadows, out
of the fierce Arizona sun on this May day of 1881. She
stepped into the dust of Allen Street, and let the faint
breeze begin to erase the sweat that had darkened the armpits of her white dress. Behan's attention was entirely
upon her. She did that to certain men. She was not particularly beautiful, but striking, with bold chestnut hair
now largely concealed under her broad-brimmed white
straw hat. She turned her back to Behan, a deliberate gesture fraught with messages. The jehu and Wells Fargo
agent were unloading the boot, where her two items of
luggage nestled.

Duvall was not her real name, but she used it with
some success in her field, where French names opened
doors. It had been the name of her lover, Jean Duvall. The
late Jean Duvall, but few people knew that either. Before
that she had been married to a dull Army lieutenant, Jason
Keogh, but he had divorced her . . . for adultery.

She bent her thoughts away from that. Her two pieces
of luggage descended to the dirt of the street. One was a
routine pebbled black leather portmanteau; the other a curious oblong case that always aroused curiosity. It held
the oilcloth faro layout, the faro box, casekeeper, numerous unopened decks of plain-backed cards, and several
chip trays.

She eyed the luggage, knowing she would need a porter, and that was when Behan glided in.

"Help you, ma'am?"

The sheriff stood before her, darkly Irish, of medium height, a man with knowing eyes and a face full of question marks and lust.

"Why, you're the sheriff. Perhaps you can recommend a hotel."

His gaze surveyed her, and she understood that he was not merely assessing the obvious costliness of her attire. He had instantly discovered the thing she tried so hard to conceal, the thing that only a connoisseur of women would unearth. Not even her high-necked and prim dress could conceal her one vulnerability from eyes such as his. He had known nothing about her, but suddenly knew everything.

That figured. Sheriff Behan was a Democrat. Laura Duvall had formulated an iron law of life: Republican gents were bad lovers but were good at business, while Democrat males knew everything there is to know about pleasing a woman but couldn't do anything else with their feckless lives. John Behan was a case in point. She knew that in five minutes he would turn her to pudding, and that he was dangerous, and that she must avoid him and get on with her mission.

"The Cosmopolitan Hotel, I think. It would be suitable for a lady of your sort."

"Thank you. You may take my bags there," she said, faintly enjoying the imperial command.

"And whom do I have the honor of welcoming to town?"

"Laura Duvall," she said.

His eyes registered nothing.

"I am Sheriff Behan, at your service," he said.

"No doubt about it," she said.

He plucked up her bags, obviously curious about the oblong one. "What do you do?" he asked.

"Gamble."

"A lady gambler. Well, I know a few parlors where you'd be welcome."

"I rarely am unwelcome."

He steered her into the hotel, which stood only a few doors away, and waited while she negotiated a room.

"You're in luck," he said. "Usually it's full. It's not the cheapest place in town either."

He was fishing. She smiled.

"Thank you, Mr. Behan. I'm sure we'll be running into each other soon."

Behan stood there, trying to prolong the meeting, but finally smiled and retreated into the heat.

The clerk helped her to her second-floor room.

Her expense money from William was adequate, but it wouldn't allow her to stay in this sort of quarters for long unless she got very lucky. The Pinkertons did not pay their agents well. He had sent her here to find out what she could about the rampant lawlessness in Cochise County. He had wanted a detailed telegraphic report in a fortnight, if possible. They had worked out a code and an address that would keep the report and its recipient entirely private.

Somebody wanted to untie the Gordian knots of Cochise County, but William refused to tell her who his client was.

"It's best if you don't know. Keep an open mind. Look at all sides. Use your charms."

She knew what he had meant.

"Each side is pointing fingers at the other. All we know is that rustling is rampant; murder so commonplace that it is scarcely noted in the local papers; and Wells Fargo coaches carrying bullion from the silver mines are robbed so frequently that the losses for the insurers, Wells Fargo, and the mines are rocketing. Death is in the air down there."

"It's Wells Fargo then."

"I'm not at liberty to say, and don't assume anything. I will tell you one thing: Wells Fargo already has a private agent in Tombstone."

And that was all she could get out of him.

This would be rather easy. She would report to William in a fortnight, maybe less. Women had their ways. William had alluded to that without ever saying it. Damned puritan hypocrite. She already knew the cast of characters, thanks to some elaborate preparation in the Chicago offices of the Pinkerton Detective Agency. All she needed was to start some men talking.

She doffed her muslin dress, poured water from the pitcher into the bowl, and gave herself a spit-bath. The tepid water felt like heaven. Twenty minutes later, she was ready for Tombstone. With luck, she might have her game going before nightfall.

Odd how she already liked the town even before examining it closely. It had the effrontery to put on cosmopolitan airs, even if it had mushroomed out of desert wastes in barely three years. It was all veneer, like the flocked blood-red wallpaper that hid the rude planks of this ramshackle building. It was a gaudy fake of a burg, and reminded her of herself.

She liked Johnny Behan, and wished she didn't. What sort of man met the arriving coaches just to womanize? She liked to be womanized, and that was the trouble. The Pinkertons didn't know that.

Like most Arizona towns, this one slumbered through the midday heat. Tonight it would come alive and kill a few more people. She didn't like daylight anyway. But she would have to brave the sun now, and try to set herself up.

She finished her ablutions, dabbed lilac between her breasts, and headed into the blistering heat. Her objective was the Oriental, less than a block away, the best saloon and gambling emporium in Tombstone, and the locus of high rollers. Wyatt Earp had a piece of the action there. Lou Rickabough, Dick Clark, and Bill Harris ran the gambling operation, and had given Earp a quarter interest mainly to protect the place. The other side, the Cowboys and Behan, were scheming to shut it down.

Earp was a Republican, damn him. He wouldn't know the first thing about women, and worse, wouldn't care.

She walked through the open double doors and into gloom. Her first impression of the Oriental was one of ornate melancholia. A gorgeous mahogany-and-white marble bar dominated one side. Light from the front doors faded swiftly, and to the rear, where the solemn gambling tables lay, the darkness was pervasive. But she could make out a handsome blue-and-gold Brussels carpet, and extravagant glass chandeliers above. At night it would be different, but by day, the Oriental was as forlorn as a cemetery. The place was almost empty, which was what she expected mid-afternoon of a weekday.

The rank odor of smelly armpits told her men were about somewhere in there. She made out assorted bodies once her eyes adjusted. Only one table was operating, a faro outfit with a small dim lamp burning above it. It had no customers.

But closer at hand, at a marble bar table, sat several dead-faced men she identified at once, again from assorted tintypes she had scrutinized. Wyatt Earp and Morgan. Lou Rickabough. Dapper Luke Short, looking like a Manhattan swell but far more deadly. They were sipping fizzy phosphates.

Good.

"You looking for something, ma'am?" The sepulchral voice emanated from the mustachioed bartender she knew to be Frank Leslie, an enigmatic gunman. Was it the faint redolence of burnt gunpowder that stamped the Oriental as the most memorable sporting palace she had ever been in?

"Yes, the owners of the gambling concession."

The bartender nodded her toward the sole occupied table.

Rickabough stood.

"You come to reform Tombstone, ma'am?"

"I deal."

"No women," said Wyatt Earp.

She stared at the Illinois man. Big, slim, blond, ice-blue eyes, and a gaze that would frost a windowpane. He stared back, his eyes measuring her for God knows what. Probably a black enameled coffin. He was not visibly heeled. Her pulse quickened. What was it about him?

"That's a little quick," she said. "I bring trade."

"Women are trouble."

She turned to portly, graying Rickabough, one of the owning partners. "I'm Laura Duvall. I'll improve your trade. Do you want profits or not?"

Earp remained quiet this time.

"We don't need anyone, Miss Duvall."

"Mrs."

"Ah, yes, but recently widowed. New Orleans, right?" She nodded.

"Aw, Wyatt, we need some action," said Morgan, admiring her with a bedroom stare. He oozed youthful enthusiasm, and she wondered how long he would let his cautious older brother dominate him.

"We've some safety concerns," Rickabough said. "If Mr. Earp is not inclined to let you run a table, then I'll have to acquiesce, as much as I'd be inclined to try out so comely a lady."

She didn't dislike him.

Wyatt continued to stare. "No women in here, but I'll buy you a sarsaparilla," he said. "Then you'll take your trade elsewhere."

Rickabough looked unhappy, but said no more.

"I made a temperance oath," she said. "No lips that touch sarsaparilla will ever touch mine. You sure you won't change your mind?"

Morgan snickered.

Wyatt never answered, but turned to the others. They had been discussing the recent perforation of some tinhorn called Charlie Storms by Luke Short, and returned to it. The perfume of gunpowder was what seduced Earps. They never noticed the cologne between her breasts.

She stood on one foot and then the other, but the employment interview had terminated. That damned Wyatt Earp.

No women.

She hurried out. The dead heat slapped her. She headed across Fourth Street and plunged into the Crystal Palace, and found it better lit from side windows. It boasted a made-in-France brass and porcelain chandelier, chased brass spittoons, and a gaudy cherry-wood bar with a fat lady, naked save for a diaphanous something or other crawling over her thick thighs, gazing down from a gilt frame.

She approached the keep, a mustachioed bald spaniel with pop eyes.

"Who runs the games?"

"We don't serve women," the keep said.

"I said who runs the games? I deal."

"Forget it. He don't allow women behind the tables. You want to play, that's okay. You want to deal, you go down the street."

"I'll come back and ask him tonight."

The keep shrugged.

What the hell. Tombstone was a man's world.

She knew better than to try Jim Earp's Sampling Room, so she headed along Allen to the Alhambra, and got the same story. No distaff dealers. They'd once let Poker Annie play a high-stakes game for fifty-one hours, but she was so ugly no one got into a fight over her, the keep explained.

She did no better at the Occidental. In fact, worse. The slick-haired tinhorn told her to set up shop in the sporting district. She could run a game there.

"I may be a sporting lady," she said, "but not on my back. I deal sitting up."

"You can sport with me sitting up," he said.

She was used to it.

They were all as bad as the Earps. Tombstone had no room for women. For the first time since she arrived, she began to fret about her mission. Her employer wanted facts. If she couldn't siphon them off the gaming tables, she would have to think of something else. But what?

She hiked back to the Cosmopolitan, wanting to lick her wounds and think. Bill Pinkerton had given her a couple of small jobs, but this was her first big one, and she didn't want to disappoint him.

She had known the Pinkertons for years. Family friends. She had grown up in flossy circles on Chicago's North Shore, the daughter of a Great Lakes steamboat magnate. She had been given everything a young lady could want, and had made her debut to introduce her to polite society and potential husbands.

But she wasn't made for polite society. They had called her brazen and reckless back then, and several swains backed out of marriages at the eleventh hour. She couldn't help it. She had no intention of being the mistress of some dull brick pile on Lake Michigan full of whining children.

So much happened, so fast, that she could barely remember the whirligig. She had gotten herself disinherited after one wild episode, married an Army captain during one of her occasional respectable interludes, found herself divorced and in bed with a New Orleans gambler, and learned the trade only to have him succumb to a lead pill that erupted from a rival's derringer. Then she was on her own, and that was when William Pinkerton, who knew her well and had kept track, recruited her.

"Laura," he said, "you're perfect for us. At home in any situation. At home in a mansion or a yacht, at home in a casino, at home with the demimonde. At home with any sort of man."

The latter had been said delicately. Her conquests were legend. She had permitted herself a wry smile. Sleuthing would be entertaining, and being entertained was more important than money, except when she had none. She planned to give Bill Pinkerton about a hundred times his money's worth.

Her treatment at the Oriental rankled. If Wyatt Earp had the slightest understanding of the ways of the world, he would have shown her some respect. From her very first glance she had known she would do anything, be anything, for Wyatt Earp, and she loathed herself for it.

She knew that the worse he treated her, the harder she would try to seduce him. She knew all about him. He had stolen some theatrical tramp named Josie Marcus from Sheriff Behan, and that was one of the reasons Tombstone smoldered. A Juliet was usually at the bottom of gang wars, and Tombstone was about to be torn apart by one.

She intended to knock Wyatt Earp down a few pegs, and maybe the way to do it was already at hand. She had caught the eye of the sheriff, and that was an ace of hearts.

Much to her surprise, Sheriff Behan was sitting there in the small lobby. He rose smoothly as she entered.

"Ah, it's Mrs. Duvall. How did it go?"

"I think you already know."

He smiled. The man was as smooth as baby flesh. "Lawmen do hear things," he said. "It seems our sporting establishments have no room for a lady."

"A woman, you mean. Whether I'm a lady is debatable."

"A lady," he said. "It's a man's town, all right. How did matters proceed at the Oriental?"

"Mr. Wyatt B.S. Earp would have no part of me."

"How do you know his middle initials?"

"I live in the sporting world."

He smiled again. Butter lips, she thought. "Perhaps you are better off not working there."

"Why?"

"Oh, the Earps are not appreciated in some quarters."

"Your quarters."

He smiled once again. He was the smilingest sheriff she had ever met.

"You have something against him," she said. Like an actress named Josie.

His smile retreated for a moment. "I will help you if you wish."

"Maybe."

"Come along. I'll talk with certain friends at the Crystal Palace. I'll tell them that a woman dealer is good for trade. You'll suck the players right out of Rickabough's place, a looker like you. What shall I offer? You run your own table and they get a quarter of your take? That's the usual."

She nodded. The man had been around.

It took only moments. Behan talked to the proprietor, a man named Frank, and Frank talked to her, and she nodded, and she was invited to set up her table in a place that reminded her of a New Orleans mortuary.

"Give the Oriental a little competition," Frank said.

"There you are, Mrs. Duvall," said Behan. "A table and a living. You may thank me by letting me take you to dinner at the Maison Dore. Fine food, best this side of San Francisco."

She agreed. Behan didn't waste a minute.

"You gonna start tonight?" Frank asked.

"Don't copper the bet," she replied.

The gaudy French restaurant astonished her. Johnny Behan astonished her too. It would cost him a week's salary to feed her there. Plainly, wearing the badge was a lucrative business.

She waited until they were knife-deep in filets mignons before opening up certain lines of inquiry.

"I don't think I like Wyatt Earp," she said.

"So I heard."

"Then you already know the story. We don't want women, he said, and that was it. I was dealt out."

"That's what I heard."

"You have funnels for ears. Come on, Johnny Behan, tell me who runs Tombstone."

He smiled again, as if life were a secret.

They drifted through four courses, but not until the chocolate mousse did Sheriff Behan pitch the deal.

"You need protection," he said. "Single woman. I'll make sure you're unharmed and free to run your game for one quarter of the take. . . ."

She smiled and awaited the rest. A man like Behan would give her options.

Two spoonfuls of mousse later, he offered her the rest.

"Of course, you could always live with me."

"Pay you your quarter? And pay that Frank his quarter? And pay Cochise County and Tombstone taxes for my table? That's another quarter. So I keep about a quarter of my winnings? That'd break the bank. The odds are no good."

"I am very skilled at what I do," he said softly.

She turned into pudding.

"I will decide after looking at your rooms and I hear the rest of your offer."

He nodded.

He led her through dead desert dusk to Toughnut Street, where he maintained a small shiplap-sided cottage with spindle gingerbread. That was luxury in a boomtown like Tombstone. Within, she discovered lace curtains on each window, doilies strewn promiscuously over the horsehair furniture, a bathing closet with a claw-foot tub, sink and running water, and an unused dead kitchen with a zinc sink. The bedroom contained a single four-poster marital bed with a bedpan under it. A privy stood at the rear corner of the lot.

"Well?"

"Where is my bed?"

"You get me in the bargain."

She laughed, not unhappily. "I don't sell myself."

"My cut for protecting you is one fourth—unless you

move in. You move in and there's no game table taxes
either. You keep everything except for Frank's cut."

Damn him. Damn him. He had ferreted her out and he
was right. "All right, I'll try it. We'll see. Don't count on
anything. Move my stuff from the hotel. I'm going to deal
tonight, and after that, I'll be here."

He wasn't going to see her in this room again until two
or three in the morning.

"I will do that," he said.

She had her table running by nine. A crowd gathered
to buck the tiger—and have a gander. She invited the
gander with a décollete neckline. The players stood three
deep, and she was reaping a fat profit as she pulled the
turns out of the faro box. At times, she saw Behan gazing
her way. At other times, she discovered various Earps,
especially Wyatt, peering dead-eyed at her and her spec-
tacular trade. The gents from the Oriental didn't look a
bit happy.

A shrewd jowly player, probably another tinhorn, kept
doubling on his losses until she pointed at the sign saying
there was a twenty-five-dollar limit, and then he got angry
and began baiting her. Behan materialized out of nowhere.

"You heard the lady," he said.

The player turned and found himself staring at the steel
circlet. He withdrew fifteen one-dollar blue chips, leaving
twenty-five, and won on a coppered seven. He was still
behind, but picked up his money and retreated, still under
Behan's steady gaze.

Laura Duvall sighed.

In the dead of the night, she discovered the sheriff was
as much a killer in bed as a ladies' man, and that was
going to ruin her judgment, damn Democrat Johnny Behan all to hell.

That's how it went. But she learned nothing of con-
sequence, except the names of those who came to visit
Sheriff Behan. Whatever they said, they said far from her
ears. Even so, the events of the next weeks bore out what

information the Pinkertons already had: Behan's associates were the "Cowboys," as the mob of reckless outlaws from the adjoining ranches were called. The Clanton boys, the Laury boys, John Ringo, Curly Bill Brocius, a dozen more hard and murderous men. They all smiled politely at her, if she happened to be around, and led the sheriff off into the dusty streets. Behan spent a lot of time talking in a dead whisper to Harry Wood, editor of *The Nugget*, the Democrat paper that loudly defended them and Sheriff Behan, and assailed the Earps and Doc Holliday.

It dawned on her that the odds were staggering. The Earp brothers, and Holliday, and maybe a couple others, against a dizzying mob of fifty or sixty, every one of them skilled with deadly weapons, full of brag, and without even the tatters of conscience.

Boozy Harry Wood made every effort to lay the blame for ongoing holdups, stagecoach robberies, rustling, and mayhem at the door of the Earps, while Mayor John Clum's Republican *Epitaph* returned the fire, but less effectually. The Cowboys spent their ill-gotten loot liberally, and made friends everywhere, especially in the whorehouses.

She heard talk of murder, revenge, triumph.

So they were going to kill the Earps and throw Holliday's emaciated corpse to the dogs. It was all coming clear. There were badges enough all around: The Earps had a deputy federal marshal badge and a city marshal badge. The Cowboys had a sheriff's badge. Legal murder.

The novelty of a woman faro dealer drew a lusty crowd every night. As word got around the moribund outlying ranches, players drifted to the Crystal Palace and stood three deep at her table, waiting for the chance to play. That pleased her. She was bleeding trade from the Oriental, and making Wyatt Earp rue his words. A striking lady with a low neckline drew more players than some grease-haired tinhorn with soiled cuffs and tobacco-stained teeth.

Johnny Behan hovered around in the background, his

meaty presence discouraging the toughs from trying to snatch her bank or cheat her or bully her with fake grievances. No sooner had a fortnight passed than the Crystal Palace was the hottest gambling emporium in Tombstone, every night awake. She opened at three in the afternoon, and rarely closed up before two in the morning, and the afternoons were her only slow moments.

That was when a woman named Kate drifted in and began playing during the sunlit afternoons when no one else was around. Laura liked her looks. Kate had a magnificent nose, thin and long and prominent, curved like a raptor's beak, an eagle nose, a noble nose that made her look royal. She spoke with a subtle accent that Laura discovered was Hungarian.

"I am John Henry Holliday's lover," Kate said one afternoon. "I have come to tell you things."

"Tell me?" Something froze in Laura. Had she been uncovered?

"I will tell you for my own reasons, even if you are Johnny Behan's woman."

"Why tell me anything? Keep your own counsel. If it's anything against Johnny, I don't want to hear it."

"Johnny is a famous lover. Not like the Earps."

Kate played a chip on a king, and Laura drew a turn. The king lost.

"Don't ever got hooked up with the Earps," she said. "At least not Wyatt. He uses women and throws them out."

"I have no intention. And why don't you talk about something else?"

"Because Wyatt is looking at you. He comes over here and watches you and thinks you don't notice."

"Mostly I don't. I keep my eyes on the board. You can't run a faro game any other way."

"What Johnny Behan has, Wyatt wants. He stole his Josie from Behan and kicked out his poor drunken Mattie. Now he's going to steal you."

Laura smiled. "Is this what you came to warn me about?"

"Yes. And not to believe a word, not one word, that Johnny Behan says about Doc or any of them."

Kate peered about sharply, afraid she had been overheard. She put five chips on the eight and coppered it. Laura drew a king and a four and adjusted the cases. Kate let her bet ride.

"Come to me if you want to know anything," Kate said. "I know everything."

Laura's caution welled up again. "About what?"

"About anything."

Laura yawned, drew a seven and six, and shuffled the deck, pulled the soda and hock, and laid them face-up under the deck, and placed it in the faro box. Then she adjusted the cases and awaited Kate's play.

Laura kept her curiosity in check. "The only thing that interests me is my game," she said.

"Not Johnny?"

"It's cheaper than the Cosmopolitan—and paying the cut he wanted."

"So is Doc's room."

They laughed.

"What's Doc like?" Laura asked.

"A Southern gentleman, fragile, sad, quick-tempered, and self-obsessed because consumption is killing him. He uses me. But I love him and always have. Is that strange?"

"No, not strange. Is he solvent?"

"Almost always. Cards are a living. He can't practice dentistry any more. Not consumptive. But when he's broke, that's what he does until he's got a new stake."

"Why do the Cowboys say he robbed a stagecoach?"

"He's too sick to rob a child of candy. I beg of you, don't listen to Johnny Behan."

"Why does Johnny Behan say it then?"

"Because Wyatt Earp stole that slut actress from him, and Doc is a friend of the Earps."

Laura smiled and cleaned Kate's five chips off the board. She had drawn a pair of eights, and all ties went to the house.

Kate sighed, and vanished toward the blind-bright doorway, and the Crystal Palace went dead.

With a little encouragement, Doc Holliday's woman would divulge much of what Laura needed to know.

The next day, Wyatt Earp sat down at her table, hulking over it as if he owned it. He had obviously waited for the moment when no other players were around. He exuded a faint malice, and she found herself loathing him. He bought a stack of dollar chips, laid one on the deuce, and coppered it.

She shuffled the deck, pulled the soda and hock, and stuffed it into the faro box. The first turn produced a seven and two. She pulled the chip off the table.

"You're costing us business," he said.

"That's good to know."

"What would it take to get you to leave?"

"I'm happy where I am."

If she had disliked him before, she hated him now. The man was a cool, assessing bully.

"You're Behan's lady."

She reddened slightly. "You're wrong on both counts."

He ignored it. "You're Behan's spy. Everything said at this table siphons into his big Irish ears, along with all your winnings."

"I'm glad you think so," she said. "And if I am, what's it to you? Here's Laura Duvall, setting up shop in the Crystal Palace because Wyatt Earp didn't want her in the Oriental. Here's Duvall, ending up with Sheriff Behan because Wyatt Earp wouldn't let her make an honest living in Tombstone. I tried every saloon in town and they all said no, and now I know why. Virgil made threats."

"You'd better be on the next stage out of town."

"I knew I was going to despise you. Play, dammit. Only players sit at my table."

"It doesn't matter to me what women think."

"Oh? Is that so? What I think is that Sheriff Behan's a crook. He lives pretty high on a sheriff salary, and I can't say I admire the gang he runs with. The only thing good about him is his way with women. He's a Democrat, and Democrats know how to pleasure ladies. I've yet to meet a Republican who was any good at it. He's a better man than you."

That sure as hell froze Deputy U.S. Marshal Earp to his stool.

"Still want me to leave?"

"Yes."

"Just try it."

He grinned suddenly and unexpectedly. "Maybe I will."

"You're a sonofabitch, Wyatt Earp."

Earp drifted into silence. A poxed cowboy, actually one of Behan's crowd, settled down, bought some chips, and began playing.

"I'll cash these," said Earp. "Cowshit's pretty thick around here."

She gave him eleven dollars.

That's how it stood. She was about to be booted out of Tombstone before she could finish her task. William Pinkerton was getting impatient. He'd spent a lot to put her in place, and she hadn't given him one snippet of information. The coded wires grew tart.

In the month she'd spent in Tombstone, it had all become clear enough. The Earps were brutes and greedy, but basically law-abiding and supported by the town's merchants. The Cowboys were flat-out bad men, itchy with the trigger finger, crooks, grafters, rustlers, stagecoach robbers, and ferocious executioners who didn't hesitate to rob and kill people in lonely places. The Cowboys were more fun. Behan milked the county of all that it was worth, and raked off a percentage of the gang's take, in exchange for "protection."

One other thing was obvious: The Earps, and their handful, were outnumbered about ten to one, and weren't long for this world. Every time Laura spotted Wyatt or Morgan or Virgil Earp, she knew she was observing a dead man. Any day, something would set off the whole thing, and the Earp brothers would occupy permanent addresses on Boot Hill.

Young Morgan Earp played her game now and then, mostly to look down her neck, but Virgil never sat down, and Wyatt played only to see who was buying her chips. She never saw the Earp women, and wouldn't have recognized them if they had walked in. Wyatt Earp fascinated her, and stirred something morbid in her belly she couldn't name. He used women, Kate had told her, and there was something in Laura willing to be used. He drew women to him, but would be a lousy lover. That was his paradox. It really didn't matter. Sometime, unless the Earps packed up, they would be lying cold and pickled in that glass-walled hearse that paraded down Allen Street a couple times a week.

She encountered Doc Holliday only once or twice, and knew that he wasn't long for the world either. Death lay in his gaze, and if consumption didn't take him soon, he would try to hasten the matter by provoking a quarrel of his own. But she could see why her friend Kate, with the big nose, put such store in him. That frail, tragic, honor-bound man was like a bird with a broken wing.

Then the kid, Morgan, quit playing at her table, and then Virgil began nabbing patrons of the Crystal Palace for public drunkenness and fining them eleven dollars. Then they announced a ridiculous new rule: no women in saloons. Laura knew it was aimed dead square at her, and it was because she was cleaning up. She had taken half the trade away from the Oriental, and the Earps had finally decided to do something about it.

"You're my protector, so do something," she said to Johnny.

"I don't enforce city ordinances, Laura. I can't. I'm a county officer. It's up to Virgil Earp."

"So tell the Earps to get the hell out of the way."

He stared at her, and she realized he was dead afraid of them. Johnny the Protector wasn't protecting her.

"Guess I'll move on," she said. "Frank says I got to pack up the game and never come back to the Palace."

"No, stay."

"It's called whoring."

"What is?"

"My favors for your support. No thanks. I've got better things to do. I like the action."

"Suit yourself."

That was dead-hearted Johnny Behan for you.

She packed up her rig at the Crystal Palace, paid Frank his quarter of the last night's deadfall, and stepped across the clay of Fifth Street and into the Oriental.

"You're not supposed to be in here," said Bill Harris.

"I won't be long. Where's the iceberg?"

"The who?"

"Wyatt."

"Taking lunch at his brother's saloon."

That meant crossing Allen Street, which she did, managing not to dip her hem in manure.

He was in there.

"Don't tell me I can't be in here, damn you."

He shrugged. Virgil, off in a corner, started to get up.

"I'll deal for you in the Oriental," she said. "Quit putting women out of saloons and I'll earn you more money than you ever saw before."

For once, that damned Wyatt Earp smiled. She didn't know how it was possible because he lacked the proper facial muscles.

"No. You should get out of here."

"Why?"

Earp peered about. A pair of rummies sat at the far

end of the bar, talking to each other. He turned his back to them and lowered his voice.

"Because William wants you to."

She froze. "What are you talking about?"

"You stayed too long. They want the report. You should have wired it two weeks ago."

"You don't make any sense," she said, fearing that he made all too much sense.

"William Pinkerton asked us to boot you out of Tombstone."

"Wyatt Earp, you think you know something but you don't."

"You did a good job. Got right in bed with the Democrats."

She reddened.

"Miss Duvall, sweetheart, did you imagine that Republican President Garfield would hire the Republican Pinkertons to look into some political rivalry in the Territory without knowing in advance which side to support? Did you think they were going to turn their backs on the Republican Earps?"

She absorbed that. "I was working for the Garfield Administration?"

"You sure were. They'd heard that Tombstone was getting a bit frolicsome, and the president thought to run in the Army or something. But first they needed facts. They turned to your Chicago friends to get them."

"And?"

"William sent you hither."

"And?"

"Instructed us to make sure you set up in the right shop. The Oriental isn't the right place. We hardly see a Cowboy in there. So we had to nudge you a little. Push you into the arms of Johnny Behan. Get you a table in a Cowboy hangout. Get you out of Tombstone when you overstayed."

"And?"

"It worked fine. Go wire your report. You know exactly who's rustling and robbing and killing around here. William's going to be pleased with it. Then catch the next train East."

It angered her. William Pinkerton had set up the whole deal. The president would get a report he could put to good use.

"You look unhappy. Jimmy, give her a sarsaparilla."

"The hell with you, Wyatt Earp," she said.

He laughed. "Have a drink."

"It was a sham. The whole thing was a sham. William sent me down here for nothing."

"No, for something. He could truthfully tell the president he had an operative here and she had laid the troubles to the Cowboys."

She had never been angrier. Swiftly, she came to some decisions. That swine William Pinkerton wouldn't get a report from her. Not one damned word. In fact, he would never see her again. And she wasn't returning to Chicago. She'd head for Leadville and set up her game. The big play in Tombstone had supplied her with a fat bank, two thousand dollars. She'd take on the high rollers up in Colorado, and enjoy it. Johnny Behan, crook and grafter that he was, had treated her with ten times more respect.

She smiled suddenly. "You've got one thing wrong, Wyatt. I've been in bed with Republicans."

Nate's Revenge

by Robert J. Conley

Robert Conley's sympathetic, powerful characters are often men forced to straddle two worlds, the white man's and the Cherokee's. His own heritage makes him eminently qualified to explore how this shaped men and women in the American West. His novels are noted for their strong characterization and plotting, often straying from the straight Western story into detective fiction or even humor, which is evidenced most strongly in his short fiction. He has studied his heritage for most of his life, and held positions in several universities and Native American Indian Studies programs throughout the West.

NATE CROWLEY STEPPED out of the stage into the main street of Tombstone. It was a busy street, crowded and loud with traffic. He had read about Tombstone. He knew that it was a busy town because of the silver mining, but he was still surprised at the bustle and the bluster. His one small bag landed beside his feet and stirred up a cloud of dust. He bent to pick it up, looked around for a likely place to sleep, then headed for the nearest rooming house. He didn't stay long in the room, just long enough to deposit his small bag. He left again, headed for the nearest saloon.

Nate thought that all eyes would be on him as he walked into the booze hall. He was a stranger. He was a snappy dresser, in a smart three-piece suit, and he was nearly six feet tall. But as he stepped into the crowded establishment, he was surprised that no one seemed to even notice him. He couldn't decide whether he was relieved or disappointed. His common sense told him that it was best this way. He didn't really want to call attention to himself. He walked to the bar and ordered a whiskey.

He was pleased to note that he could keep his back to the room and, leaning on the bar, could study a large part of the big room in the long mirror behind the bar. He wanted to get a look at all the faces if he could, but he wanted to do so without calling any attention to himself. He sipped his whiskey, because he wanted to keep a clear head. He had only ordered the drink so no one would question his presence in the saloon.

He was looking for Ira Long. He had good reason to believe that Ira would be in Tombstone, and he had endured a long, expensive, and uncomfortable trip for just that reason. It had been seven years since he had seen Ira, and he hoped that he would recognize Ira before Ira saw and recognized him. He meant for all the surprise to be on his side. He meant to kill Ira. It was almost all he had thought about for these last seven years. It was all he had lived for. It meant everything to him.

As he sipped his whiskey, Nate glanced from one face to another in the mirror. None were familiar. But he knew that somewhere in this town, he would find Ira. His mind wandered back to that time seven years ago, that time that had changed his entire life, that time that now defined the meaning of his life, that time when he and Ira had been the best of friends. In those days, Nate would have gladly laid down his life for his friend. He very nearly had. He had given five years, but in the process, he had also learned that Ira had a very different view of friendship than his own.

They had been fun-loving young men, more than a bit
wild. They had met punching cows on a ranch in New
Mexico, and they had hit it off at once. Both young men
liked drinking, chasing women, a good fistfight, and
shooting. There was no malice in it, just good, clean fun.
They were a little rowdy, Nate admitted to himself, but
then, so were most of the cowboys he knew, and none of
them meant any harm, and for the most part, no one ever
got hurt, at least not badly.

But then there had come a time when the punchers'
pay just didn't go far enough for the two fun-loving cowboys. There was never enough money for the fun they
pursued. They tried gambling, but they lost more than
they won and made their problem even worse than it had
been before. The whiskey and the women cost money. So
did the bullets. The only thing they enjoyed that was free
was a fistfight. They had to do something. They talked it
over and decided on a life of crime.

Their first job had been a stagecoach holdup. It netted
them a few hundred dollars, and they decided that it had
hardly been worth the risk. So they robbed a store. It
wasn't much better. They decided they would rob banks,
and for a while they got away with it. They had more
money than they could spend, but their identities became
known, and they had to hit the trail.

They had a few thousand dollars with them, all in
Nate's saddlebags, when the posse got on their trail. It
had slipped up on them somehow. Even seven years later,
Nate was more than a little embarrassed about that fact.
They should have noticed such a large posse much sooner.
So many men and horses should not have gotten so close
to them without some kind of warning. But they had, and
the two partners in crime had mounted up to run for it.
The posse had been close behind, close enough for some
of the posse to start shooting from the saddle as they rode.

It's a tough thing to get off a good shot while riding
on the back of a running horse, but one of the lawmen's

shots got Ira's horse, and sent Ira sprawling in the trail. Nate reined in his mount and looked back. There was Ira in the dirt, and not far behind him the posse was closing the gap fast. It was crazy to think of going back for Ira. It was crazy to think of trying to outrun them with two men on a horse. But Ira was his partner, and Nate didn't think. He only reacted. He rode back, reached down, and helped Ira onto the back of his horse. Bullets from the fast-approaching posse whizzed past them as Nate whipped up the horse again. Ira looked over his shoulder.

"They're catching up, Nate," he shouted. "It's all over for us."

"Shut up," Nate yelled back. "We'll get out of this together, or we'll go down together. Sling some lead their direction. That might slow them down."

Ira slipped the six-gun out of his holster.

"Sorry, Nate," he said, "but this riding double will never do."

He banged the barrel of his revolver down on Nate's head, but it struck only a glancing blow, painful nonetheless, and dizzying. Nate struggled with the fuzziness in his head from the surprising blow and from the even more surprising source of the blow. Then Ira hit him again and pushed him from the saddle. Nate hit the road hard, bouncing and rolling. The next thing he knew, he was being manhandled by members of the posse. Ira was long gone—with Nate's horse and with all the money. Five years in prison had followed for Nate. It had taken two more years for him to get a little money together and to get some word of the whereabouts of Ira Long.

Those seven years had seemed like a lifetime to Nate, but at last they were over. The source of his information was good. He trusted it absolutely. He knew that Ira was in Tombstone, and he knew that he would see him soon. Then he would even the score. It wasn't just that someone had knocked him in the head and stolen his horse and all his money. It wasn't just that someone had let him take the rap and had gotten away clean. It was that *Ira* had done all these things to him. Ira, his best friend, his partner, had done all that, and he had done it after Nate had endangered himself by going back to help Ira. If it had been someone else, it wouldn't have mattered all that much. But it had been Ira, and there was no forgetting or forgiving that.

Nate took another sip of his whiskey, and he noticed that the bartender shot him a glance. It occurred to him that he might be irritating the bartender by drinking so slowly, but he had no intention of gulping the stuff. He continued searching the crowd, studying the faces in the mirror. He saw nothing familiar in any of them. The far side of the room to his right was beyond his vision in the reflection, so, having scrutinized all he could by looking over the bar, he turned casually, his drink in his right hand, his left elbow resting on the bar, and he looked toward that end of the room. There was no sign of Ira. Leaving half his drink in the glass, he left the bar.

He hit four more saloons using the same technique and with the same results. He thought that he could spend a month just casing the saloons in Tombstone. He had never seen a town with so many such establishments. It was hard for him to believe, even with the busy streets, that one town could support so many. It was a tedious job he had given himself, but he could think of no other way to locate Ira. In spite of his sipping and not finishing his drinks, he was beginning to feel the effects of the alcohol. His capacity for booze had diminished considerably during his five years in prison, and in the two years following, he had not managed to regain it. He went to his room to sleep.

Nate's sleep was troubled and fitful that night. It was filled with images of Ira. Some of the images were happy. They were images of the early days, the days when the two young men had been inseparable friends, happy and carefree, drinking, chasing women, brawling in saloons, robbing stagecoaches, banks, and country stores and spending money lavishly and wildly. Then they changed to the time when Ira had betrayed him. They were riding double on Nate's horse, the posse close behind. Ira pounded Nate on the head with his pistol and threw him off the racing horse. He landed hard, bounced and rolled, over and over again.

Then the dreams changed again. They became hopeful dreams of the future, dreams in which Nate faced a frightened Ira, and Ira dropped to his knees to beg forgiveness, to plead for his life. Nate was hard and unmoving. He drew his revolver, thumbed back the hammer, and pointed the barrel at Ira's chest. Ira cried and whimpered. Nate smiled. His finger tightened on the trigger, and he woke up in a cold sweat, only to sleep again and dream again.

The following morning, Nate got up and dressed. He left his side arm and holster in the room and pocketed a British Webley Bulldog in his right jacket pocket. He didn't want to appear to be a gunfighter or even someone looking for a fight, but he did want to be ready in case he ran across his prey. He went out to find himself some breakfast. In the street and over his meal, he studied the faces of everyone he saw. Still, there was no sign of Ira. He decided that he would have to change his tactics and start to ask questions. He had hoped to be able to just spot Ira. Asking around could backfire on him. Someone might get the word back to Ira that he was being looked for. Still, it was better than what he had been doing. He could watch and wait until all his money was spent and still not have achieved his goal. He walked over to the Oriental Saloon.

He hadn't yet gone into the Oriental. Even so, he was not going there to do what he had been doing in the other saloons. He was going to ask questions. Inside, the place was not too crowded, for it was early in the day. He went directly to the bar and leaned his elbows on it. The bartender, not busy, came right over.

"What can I do for you?" he asked.

"Can I get a cup of coffee?" Nate asked.

"Sure."

The bartender turned away to get the coffee, and when he brought it back and placed it on the bar in front of Nate, Nate tossed a coin on the bar. "Say," he said, "I'm looking for someone. An old friend of mine. Used to be my partner. I heard he was here in Tombstone, but I ain't had no luck spotting him around town. Maybe you know him. Name's Ira Long."

The bartender shook his head. "Never heard of him," he said. "Sorry."

"Well," Nate said, "there's a lot of folks in this town."

"More come in every day," the bartender said. "It's the silver mines. It brings in prospectors, gamblers, entertainers, drummers, all kinds. You might check with the marshal. Him and his brothers try to keep up with everything that goes on around here."

"Thanks," Nate said. "Where's his office?"

"It's right down the street," the bartender said, "but he's sitting right over there." He gave a nod. "That's him, Virgil Earp, and that's his brother Wyatt with him."

Nate took another slurp of coffee and put the cup down. "Thanks again," he said. He walked over to the table the bartender had indicated and found two men with handlebar mustaches, wearing black suits and visiting over coffee.

"Excuse me," he said. "Marshal Earp?"

The two Earp brothers looked up at Nate. "That's me," said Virgil. "What can I do for you?"

"My name's Nate Crowley," Nate said. "I just got into town yesterday on the stage. I'm looking for an old friend, partner of mine, name of Ira Long. I heard he was in town, and I come looking for him. I ain't seen him in seven years, and I come a long ways to find him. He was the best friend I ever had. The bartender said that if anyone would know about him, it would likely be you."

"What name did you say?" Virgil asked.

"Ira Long," said Nate.

Virgil shook his head and looked at Wyatt.

"Never heard of him," Wyatt said. "What's he look like?"

"About my size and age," Nate said. "But he's got blond hair and blue eyes. Pretty good-looking fellow. He used to get all the best-looking gals when we was running together. He's a little bow-legged, I reckon. Worked as a cowboy for a lot of years. Both of us did."

"Well, I wish we could help you," Virgil said, "but that don't call anyone to mind. Course, there's a bunch of folks in Tombstone who come to town with new names. Could be your old partner's like that, not using his right name anymore."

Nate hadn't thought of that, but it made good sense. Ira was still wanted for his part in the old robberies, and he would likely have a pretty good idea that Nate would be looking for him sooner or later. Probably Marshal Earp was right. Probably Ira wasn't using his own real name here in Tombstone. This was going to be even tougher than Nate had thought.

"You might check the claims office," Wyatt said, "and the real-estate offices. If he came to mine or if he got himself any property, they'd know about him. Course, they won't be any help if he's using a different name."

"Thanks," Nate said. "I reckon it'll be worth a try."

Nate left the saloon and started on the rounds suggested by Wyatt Earp. He had no luck in the claims office or the first two real-estate offices. He was in the third realty office, feeling like this too was a waste of time, but when he had given the man a description of Ira, the man scratched his head and wrinkled his brow in thought.

"Well, sir," he said, "I sure don't know any Ira Long, but the description sounds like it could be Mr. Thomas."

"Mr. Thomas?" Nate said, suddenly excited with hope.

"Mr. Richard Thomas," the man said. "You say it's

been seven years since you saw your friend?"

"That's right," Nate said.

"Well, Mr. Thomas has been in Tombstone for nearly that long, I'd say. He come to town and bought himself a business. Been doing right well, he has. Dry-goods store right down the street. You can't miss it. Got his name right out front on the sign. Thomas Dry Goods. Course, he might not be your friend at all, but he fits the description, all right. I can't think of anyone else."

"Thanks, mister," Nate said. "Thanks a lot."

SURE ENOUGH, THOMAS Dry Goods was easy to find. Nate stood on the board sidewalk for a while just studying the outside of the building. It had a facade like most of the other buildings along the street, and it had two large glass windows, each decorated with a variety of goods that were available inside. Up above the door and windows was a large sign with big red letters that identified the place as Thomas Dry Goods.

Old Ira's done right well for himself, Nate thought. Most likely he used the money from our last job to set himself up.

Nate seethed inside. He burned with a desire to confront Ira, to upbraid him with his cowardly act, and then to blast him to Kingdom Come. But how should he proceed? He couldn't just walk into the store and kill Ira then and there in cold blood. Surely he would not be able to escape the Earps and the sheriff, Johnny Behan. And likely Ira had new friends in this town. He had been here nearly seven years according to the real-estate man. Nate thought that perhaps he could go inside and let Ira see him. Let Ira sweat it out. Maybe he could face Ira and challenge him to a fair gunfight. That way it wouldn't be called a murder. He had thought about this moment for so many years that now that it was nigh, he couldn't decide just how to proceed.

Then he reminded himself that it might not even be Ira

in there. It was someone the people in town knew as Richard Thomas—a storekeeper. Maybe, after all, Richard Thomas was really Richard Thomas and not Ira at all. Maybe he just happened to fit the general description that Nate had given of Ira. And it was difficult to imagine Ira as a storekeeper. Nate thought about going back to the Oriental and asking the Earps about Richard Thomas. They might know if the man was really who he said he was. But then, that would be too obvious. They would want to know, if Nate's story was true, why he hadn't just gone in the store to see the man. At last he decided there was nothing to do but go inside and see for himself. He hitched his britches and walked to the door. Taking a deep breath, he opened the door and stepped inside.

There were four customers in the store, looking around at various items. A woman carried a bolt of cloth to the counter, where the clerk, also a woman, wrapped it up and collected the price from the customer. Nate looked at the woman behind the counter. She was young and beautiful. When she was no longer occupied, he walked over to the counter.

"May I help you, sir?" she asked.

"Well, yes, ma'am," Nate said, pulling his hat from his head. "I'm looking for the owner, Mr. Thomas."

"He isn't in just now," the woman said. "Perhaps I can help you. I'm Mrs. Thomas."

Nate was stunned. He hadn't expected this. Ira had a wife. If Thomas was really Ira. "No, thank you, ma'am," he said. "I really need to see Mr. Thomas. When do you expect him to be back?"

"He should be here around one o'clock," she said. "May I tell him who called?"

Nate hesitated a moment. "Oh, no, ma'am," he said. "Thank you. I'll just drop back by later."

IT SEEMED TO Nate like the longest morning of his life. Mr. Thomas might not be Ira, but then again, he might

be. And if he was, Nate was very close to him after these
long seven years, seven years of hate and anticipation and
longing for revenge. He tried to imagine the moment he
would confront Mr. Thomas and discover him to actually
be Ira. His mind constructed an actual conversation, the
things he would say to Ira and Ira's response. He tried to
picture the expression on Ira's face when Ira recognized
him, the surprise, shock, fear.

He thought about the moment when he would pull the
trigger, and he tried to imagine the expression of horror
on Ira's face as the hot lead tore into his chest. And then
his mind replayed the images from his dreams the night
before. Then he wondered where Ira—or Mr. Thomas—
might be since he was not at his store. Would he be at
home? He considered going back to the store to ask Mrs.
Thomas where he could find the man. But he discarded
that idea. He should have asked while he was there in the
store. He would feel foolish going back now to ask.

Considering it, though, put his mind back on the young
woman in the store, Mrs. Thomas. If Ira was really Mr.
Thomas, then that lovely young thing was Ira's wife. A
new image came into Nate's mind, a picture of the woman
screaming in horror at the sight of her bloody, dying husband. He wondered whether Mr. Thomas, or Ira, when he
had arrived in Tombstone nearly seven years ago, had
brought her with him, or had he met her and married her
in Tombstone? How long had they been married? Were
there children? His mind was starting to feel sorry for the
woman, but he steeled it against her. It was too bad that
she had made such a sorry choice for a husband, a cowardly bastard who would steal a horse and money from
his own partner, his best friend, even after that friend had
put himself at risk to go back and rescue him from the
fast-approaching posse.

No, he told himself. It was too bad about the little lady,
but she didn't change anything. Ira had done what he had
done, and it was a thing that could not be forgiven. It was

a thing that he must pay for, and Nate intended to make him pay in full. That thought was all that had kept him going for the last seven years. It had to be done, and that was all there was to it. It had to be done, and Nate was going to do it. He only had to wait until one o'clock. After having waited for seven long years, he could wait until one o'clock.

IRA LONG, IN his new identity as Richard Thomas, respected Tombstone merchant, arrived at the store a little early. His wife was busy behind the counter with a customer, so Ira walked around behind the counter without a word. In another moment, the customer had been taken care of and was on her way out of the store. Ira stepped over to his wife and kissed her on the cheek.

"You're early," she said.

"A little," Ira said. "The buggy's outside. You can go on home, sweetheart. I'll take over from here. Have you had a good morning?"

"Yes," she said. "Business has been brisk."

"Good." Ira said. "Well, now, you run on along home. I'll see you right after closing time."

She headed for the front door, but just before she opened it to go out, she paused and looked back over her shoulder at her husband. "Oh, Richard," she said, "there was a gentleman here earlier looking for you. He said he'd stop back by after one o'clock."

"What's his name?" Ira asked.

"He didn't say," she answered. "When I asked him, he just said that he'd stop back later. He was a nice-looking young man, and he was very polite. Well dressed."

"And he didn't say what his business was?"

"No, he didn't."

"Ah, well," said Ira. "I'll find out when he gets here. Don't worry about it. I'll see you for supper."

But when she had gone outside and shut the door, Ira's brow wrinkled. Who could be coming to see him and what was his business? Why hadn't the man given his name? What could be so mysterious? Only one possibility came to his mind, and it was the one that had been plaguing him for years, for seven years, ever since he had clubbed his partner, Nate, and left him to face the posse alone. It had been a cowardly act, but it had been an impulsive thing based only on an instinct for survival. As soon as he had done it, he had felt terrible pangs of guilt, and in seven years, time they had not left him.

Many times over the years, he had thought that he should try to make things right with Nate, but really, there was no way that could be done. While Nate had been languishing in prison, Ira could not have done anything to get him out. He could only have gotten himself thrown in, and that wouldn't have helped Nate. As time passed, Ira simply accepted that he had been a coward and that he had betrayed his best friend. He had decided that he would simply have to live with the terrible truth about himself and with the guilt that tormented him. And over the years, he had learned that he could live with it. It was a dark secret that he shared with no one, but he could live with it.

But that wasn't all. There was the fear. He had known all along that there was more than a chance that Nate would search him out. He had asked himself more than once, what would I have done had Nate done that to me? And the answer had always been the same. I would find him and kill him if it took the rest of my life. Nate had almost surely gone to jail, for the posse had been almost on their heels when Ira had dumped him off his horse. But for how long? They had done no killings, so it would not be forever. Sooner or later, Nate would be free again, and when that day came, Ira knew, Nate would be coming after him. He wouldn't know where to look, but he would be persistent. He would keep looking. And when Nate at last came, he would come looking to kill.

Ira didn't want to kill Nate. He felt guilty enough as

things stood. But neither did he want to die. For now, especially, Ira had too much to lose. He had a lovely wife with whom he was very much in love, and he had a good business. He still had a good many years of life left in him, unless his life should be cut short unnaturally. He didn't intend to let that happen if he could prevent it. He thought about closing the store, but then what would he tell his wife? And he couldn't just leave it closed indefinitely. If Nate knew where he was, he wouldn't leave town in a few days. He'd wait around. Nate would have to come back to the store sooner or later. Then he thought about strapping on a six-gun, but he decided against that too. He didn't think that Nate would be fool enough to gun down an unarmed man in the middle of the day in Tombstone.

Of course, he told himself, the man his wife had met earlier in the day might not even have been Nate. Maybe all this worry was for nothing. Even so, his heart jumped when the bell over the door jingled and a man wearing a gray suit stepped into the store. Ira looked hard at the man, and when the man straightened up and looked toward him, Ira recognized him immediately, in spite of the changes of seven hard years. For a long and tense moment, the two men stood staring at one another. At last Ira broke the uneasy silence.

"Hello, Nate," he said. "I thought it would be you. I knew you'd be coming for me sooner or later."

"I came to kill you, Ira," Nate said.

"I know," said Ira. He held his arms out to his sides. "I'm not armed."

Nate held open his jacket. "Me neither," he said, although he lied, for the Webley was in his jacket pocket. "I thought we might just get reacquainted first. It's been a long time. The killing can wait. There's no hurry."

"You think that if you wait around long enough," Ira said, "I'll get nervous and make a try for you? Is that your game? Then when you kill me you can call it self-defense."

Nate shrugged. "I don't know that I have any game," he said. "I just know that I been looking for you for a long time, and I mean to kill you."

"I ain't going to just stand still for it," Ira said. "I know I done you wrong, and I feel bad about it. I've felt guilty about what I done all these years, but I'm not going to just let you kill me for it. No matter how guilty I feel."

"I figured you'd fight me," said Nate. "I wouldn't want it any other way, even though you don't deserve no better than a shot in the back with no warning."

"I won't argue with you, Nate," said Ira. "I agree. That's what I deserve. Even so, like I told you, I won't just stand still for it. I won't just take it. I got too much to lose here, Nate. I got my wife and my business."

"A business, I reckon," said Nate, "that you got started using our money. Half of that money was mine."

"I'll give it to you, Nate," Ira said. "I've got it in the bank. I'll give you your share plus interest."

"If I just forget about what you done to me and ride out of here leaving you alive?"

"Yeah."

"I won't be bought off," Nate said. "I thought about this too many years."

The bell over the door jingled and a customer came into the store. Nate moved over against the wall and sulked until the customer found what he was looking for, paid for it, and left. Then: "Shut her up," Nate said.

"What?" said Ira.

"Close the damn store," Nate said. "We don't need no more interruptions."

"If I close—"

Nate whipped the Webley out of his pocket and leveled it at Ira. "I said close it up," he snapped.

Slowly, Ira moved around the counter and over to the door. He flipped over the sign that said OPEN on one side and CLOSED on the other. Then he locked the door. He looked back at Nate. "You said you were unarmed," he said accusingly.

"I lied," said Nate. "Is that anywhere near as bad as what you done to me?"

"What now?" Ira asked.

"Well," said Nate, "I've changed my mind. I don't want to wait around. It's no fun. I think we ought to get this thing over with. You got a six-gun and a gun belt here?"

Ira nodded affirmatively.

"Is the gun loaded?"

"Yeah."

"Show me where it's at."

Ira indicated a location under the counter, and Nate moved around and pulled out the rig. He withdrew the revolver from its holster and examined it. It was fully loaded. "Okay," he said. "Wrap it up."

"Wrap it up?"

"You heard me," Nate snapped.

Ira wrapped the gun, belt, and holster as if it were a purchase. Nate picked it up off the counter and tucked it under his left arm. "All right," he said. "Let's go."

They walked to Nate's room, where Nate got his own revolver and belt. Then they walked to the livery stable, where he made Ira rent two saddle horses. They rode out of town together, neither man speaking. At last Nate stopped them. "This ought to do," he said. There was no one in sight in any direction. Both men dismounted, and Nate tossed the wrapped package to Ira.

"Open it up and strap it on," he said.

Ira stood for a moment unbelieving. He held the package in front of him in both his arms. He looked at Nate. "You mean to make this a fair fight?" he asked.

"A gun duel," Nate said.

"You said you came to kill me," said Ira.

"That's what I came for."

"In a fair fight," Ira said, "I might kill you. You think about that?"

"I was always faster than you," said Nate.

"But not as accurate," said Ira. "And you been a long time without practice."

"I been out of jail two years," said Nate. "I've had time to get back in shape. I'm better than I used to be. How about you, storekeeper? You been practicing?"

Ira stared at Nate, still unbelieving.

"Strap the damn thing on," snapped Nate.

Ira unwrapped the rig and wrapped the belt around his waist. "Go ahead," he said. "I won't draw on you. I can't."

"What the hell do you mean?" said Nate. "You beat me over the head and stole my horse and money. You left me for the damn posse. Left me to do five years in prison while you set yourself up as an honest, respectable store-keeper and got yourself a pretty wife. You did all that to me after I went back for you. You were down. I had my horse and I had the money. I had a good lead on that posse too. But you went down, and I went back for you. After all that, you turned on me. And now you say you can't draw on me?"

"I won't," Ira said.

"You think that'll keep me from killing you?" Nate said. "Is that what you're trying to pull? You think I won't gun you down in cold blood? I will if you won't draw. If you won't go for your gun, I'll kill you anyway. I waited too many years for this. I come too far to find you."

Ira unbuckled the gun belt and let the rig fall to the ground at his feet. "Go ahead," he said. "Kill me. It won't give you back your lost years, and it won't give you back your share of our loot. But if it will ease your pain in any way, go ahead and shoot."

"Back in town," Nate said, "you told me you wouldn't stand still for this. Just what the hell are you trying to pull on me? You want to die? What about your store and your wife?"

"I thought about it all the way out here, Nate," Ira said. "We were best friends. We were partners. I put an end to all that by what I done, and it was a wrong thing for me to do. I never thought about it, Nate. I just done it before I even knew what I was doing. It was like if a lion jumped up in my path and I shot it real quick-like. You know what I mean? A reflex. There was no thought about it at all. I'm ashamed of it. I think about it every day. I dream about it. I'm living a lie. I won't add another wrong to what I done to you. I won't take a chance that I might win this fight. You might as well just go ahead and get it over with. Once you've killed me, you can strap that belt back on me. You can even fire a round or two from my six-gun. You can make it look like a fair fight, if you want to."

"Pick it up," said Nate.

"No," said Ira.

Nate slipped the revolver from his holster and pointed it at Ira's gut. "Pick it up, I said."

Ira stood silent.

"Damn it, Ira, pick up the gun."

Still, Ira stood motionless and silent, and Nate pulled the trigger sending a bullet into the dirt just by Ira's left foot. Ira didn't flinch. "Pick it up," Nate shouted. Ira didn't move. Nate fired another shot, the bullet coming dangerously close to Ira's left ear. Still, Ira did not reach down for the gun at his feet. Nate felt a moment of panic. In spite of his threats, he did not want to shoot Ira in cold blood. He wanted a fight. He wanted to best him in a duel. He had not counted on this. He didn't know what to do. A thought flashed through his mind that maybe Ira was waiting for him to empty his revolver and then kill him. But he dismissed that thought. How would Ira know that Nate wouldn't shoot him down? Then he had another thought.

"Alright, you son of a bitch," he said. "Don't fight me. I'm going to find your pretty little wife, and I'm going to tell her the whole story. I'm going to tell her your real name, and I'm going to tell her how you and me used to run whores and rob banks and such. And then I'm going to tell her what I done for you and how you turned on me. I'm going to let her know just what a cowardly bastard you really are."

He holstered his revolver and walked over to his horse. As he put his foot in the stirrup to mount up, Ira flung himself through the air, grabbing Nate, and both men fell hard to the ground and rolled in the dirt. "You stay away from her," Ira shouted, pounding a fist into the side of Nate's head.

"Ha," Nate said through clenched teeth. "I got to you, did I?" He beat at Ira's ribs with both his fists.

Ira tried to pin Nate's arms down with his own arms, and in the attempt, he felt the Webley in Nate's jacket pocket. He managed to get his hand in the pocket and pull out the Webley. He cocked it and placed the barrel against Nate's temple. "Hold it," he said.

Nate quit struggling, and Ira slowly backed off him and stood up. Carefully, he reached down with his left hand and pulled the revolver out of Nate's holster. Still pointing the Webley at Nate, he moved back to where he had left his own gun and belt on the ground, and he picked that up. "Okay," he said. "Now you can mount up."

Nate climbed into the saddle, all the while looking warily at the Webley in Ira's hand. "Where we going?" he asked.

Ira mounted up, still pointing the Webley's barrel at Nate. "We're going just where you said you were going. "We're going to my house to see my wife, but we're going on my terms, not yours. Get moving."

AGAIN THEY RODE in silence, and by the time they reached the Thomas home, it was still mid-afternoon. As far as Mrs. Thomas knew, her husband was still at the store. About a hundred yards from the house, Nate reined in.

"Keep going," said Ira.

"What are we doing here?" Nate asked. "I said I was going to tell on you. You want me to do that?"

"No," Ira said. "I'm going to tell Kate the whole story. I'm going to tell her myself. Then I'm going to tell her that you came here to kill me, and I'm going to tell her that I won't shoot it out with you. If you want to kill me, you'll just have to do it in cold blood. Once I've told her, I'll give you back your guns."

"That's crazy," Nate said. "What's that going to get you?"

"Nothing," said Ira, "but she'll know. When I'm dead, she'll know why. She'll know the truth, and at least for a little while before I die, I won't be living a lie with her anymore. Now get moving."

They rode on up to house, and Kate heard their approach and came out on the porch to see who was riding up. "Richard," she said, "what are you doing home at this hour?" She saw the gun in his hand, and her face registered fear and worry.

"Oh," said Ira. He stuck the Webley in his pocket. "It's all right. I brought an old friend to meet you, and I have something to tell you."

Kate shot a worried look at Nate, then turned back toward her husband. "What is it?" she said.

"Not much," said Nate, speaking up quickly. "Me and your husband—Richard—we used to be good friends. We punched cows together for a few years. Why, we was the best of friends, me and ole Richard here. That's why I wouldn't give you my name this morning in your store. You see, we hadn't seen each other for over seven years, and I wanted to surprise him. That's all."

"Oh," she said. "Well, will you be coming in to supper with us? It will be a little while yet. I didn't expect Richard home until after five." Her voice betrayed lingering suspicion. The story Nate had told would have seemed all right, but there was the gun that Richard had been holding when the two men first rode up.

"No, ma'am," Nate said. "Thank you just the same. You see, I have to be moving on. That's the reason Richard closed up the story early. It's the only way we'd have had any time to visit. I'm leaving town right away. I have pressing business elsewhere."

He tipped his hat, turned his mount, and started riding back toward Tombstone. He waited for a word from Ira to stop him. He waited for a gunshot that would send hot lead tearing into his back. There was nothing. He rode on a few yards, then stopped the horse. Twisting in the saddle, he looked back at the Thomases. He raised the hat off his head and waved it.

"So long, Richard," he shouted. "Ma'am, it was a pleasure meeting you."

Then he kicked the horse into a gallop and headed for town. He wondered if a stagecoach would be leaving yet before dark. If not, for sure there would be one out of town in the morning. He would be on it, no matter where it was headed.

The Fly on the Wall

by Judy Alter

Judy Alter is a modern-day stylist whose work bridges the traditional themes of Western fiction with some of the more contemporary issues of the West. Celebrated by reviewers everywhere, Judy has worked in a variety of styles and voices in both short fiction and long. She is an excellent example of the female Western writer whose time has definitely come, especially with such Spur-winning novels as *Mattie*.

THERE I WAS, pulling myself up into that fool stage to Tombstone one more time, hitching my skirts so I didn't trip, and still trying not to show my ankles so I'd get catcalls from the men standing around. When I poked my head into the coach, I looked into the prettiest green eyes I'd ever seen. The only other passenger in the coach was a young lady, and I use both those words deliberately. She wasn't yet eighteen, I didn't think, but she had all the graces of a lady, those graces I knew damn well I didn't have.

Just then my skirt caught on the step of the coach, and I heard a ripping sound. "Damn!" I said loudly, pulling myself the rest of the way into the stage. Then I remembered the young girl, and though it was unlike me, I felt just a bit ashamed of my language. I decided to try to start over.

"Mornin'," I said.

"Good morning," she said with a tentative quality about her voice. Her eyes told me she was both faintly amused and slightly shocked by my unladylike ascent into the carriage.

She wore a very proper brown traveling dress trimmed with silk ribbon, long-sleeved, tight at the waist, and uncomfortable-looking as hell. Her shoes were high-top affairs of fine leather, white on top and black for the main part of the shoe, with slightly elevated heels—I swore she couldn't walk ten feet in them, especially not on the dirt streets of Tombstone.

Her hair was pulled back and covered with a straw hat that had a brown woven affair hanging down behind it into which she'd tucked the most incredible red hair I'd ever seen. It was curly too, for stray bits escaped around her face in corkscrews.

I was conscious of the difference in our appearances—maybe even self-conscious about it. I wore a white shirt-waist—now some wrinkled and with a spot of coffee spilled on it that I'd tried and failed to get out over my breakfast—and a black broadcloth skirt, with sturdy black shoes, the only kind a sensible woman would wear in this godforsaken part of the country. My hair had been neatly piled on my head in the morning with a roll, secured by countless hairpins, framing my face. But I knew by now, in the midday heat in July, limp strands hung about my face and down the back of my neck. They didn't curl into charming corkscrews like hers did. My face was sweaty, and I had to mop it with my tired handkerchief.

I was almost struck dumb by the expression in her eyes—innocence, maybe a little fear. She was too young and too sweet—did I really use that word?—to be on a stage to Tombstone by herself.

I tried again to start a conversation. "Name's Kate, Kate Elder. They . . . they call me Big Nose Kate." There, I'd said it. The reason for the nickname was obvious, and

I usually figured I might as well get the name out in the open. It sort of kept people from staring at the prominence of that one feature. Having a big nose didn't make me ugly, and I knew that. In his rare sober moments, Doc Holliday called me a "fine figure of a woman." It didn't seem to bother him that as a good-sized woman I towered over his skinny frame.

Doc Holliday, of course, was the reason I was back on the stage one more time. Although he was only twenty-eight, I thought of Doc as an old man—that's 'cause he was dying of consumption. He was a dentist, but he didn't care much about practicing his trade—once told Allie Earp he couldn't be bothered pulling her "baby teeth" when she had a toothache. Knowin' he was dyin', Doc was one of the best shootists of the West—that was because he didn't fear dying. He was difficult, moody, unpredictable, and violent—and he was the only man I'd ever really loved in a lifetime of—well, okay, I was a few years older than him—of making my living on the frontier in ways that ladies didn't talk about. Doc and I really got together in Colorado, where he'd killed a man over a poker game—actually, he'd cut the guts out of the man, and I hated to think about it to this day. But I could tell they were fixin' to lynch him, and I got him out of that jail. No, I'm not telling how I did it. But we'd been to-gether—off and on—ever since.

When he followed the Earp brothers to Tombstone, I followed Doc—though his companions were none too pleased about it. Doc sort of set up practice as a dentist, and I . . . well, I did what I knew best how to do. I opened a "palace of pleasure"—some palace, in a canvas tent, with just swags of canvas hung down to create "private" rooms. Miners didn't care, and the five girls I hired were busy all the time. Me? I ran the business, but I spent my nights with Doc.

But about two weeks before that stagecoach ride, he and I had one of our classic rows. Doc was usually too drunk to fight by talking, but he wasn't above punching me when he got mad. And I'd just told him I wouldn't take it anymore, I was getting on the stage and going to Tucson. He'd said, "Good. Get on that damn stage and get outta my sight."

I went, but it wasn't easy. I had a business in Tombstone—matter of fact, I had a thriving business. Folks around Tombstone called it "Kate's Sporting House," even though it was only in a tent. But I even left that behind. I was that mad at Doc.

But once I was in Tucson, I began to miss that coughing, tubercular, mean son of a bitch. And when he wrote one of his flowery letters saying he missed me, I took the next stage back to Tombstone.

My traveling companion studied me, and at length said uncomfortably, "You're . . . well, it isn't that big. I . . . I didn't even notice it."

"No need to fool an old bag like me," I said. "It's a big nose. I'm used to it." I settled myself in the seat. "Ain't you a mite young to be travelin' off to a place like Tombstone by yourself?" I asked.

"No." She didn't look like she believed it herself.

"Well," I said sort of preachily, wanting to impress her with my worldly knowledge, "it's a rough place, Tombstone is. Aren't many ladies there, if you know what I mean."

If she knew, she ignored the comment. "I have business in Tombstone," she said, smoothing back one loose curl with her left hand. A diamond sparkled on her ring finger.

"You looking for a lost lover? Or, sometimes I've heard ladies say they're looking for their brother, when they really mean a lover."

She shook her head. "Neither."

I didn't believe her. The ring was a giveaway. "I'd hide that ring if I were you," I advised.

She looked at the ring and shrugged. "I shouldn't mind losing it."

Wyatt Earp used to tell Doc I was a slow thinker, but I wasn't all that slow. She wouldn't mind losing the ring, because she'd lost the one who gave it to her . . . and I bet she'd lost him to Tombstone and the many pleasures and free money that flowed there. I was beginning to know a little more about this young lady—and the more I knew, the more I worried about her. She'd never survive in Tombstone.

"Might not like the way you lose it," I said. Just then, there was the driver's loud yell, and the coach took off with a jerk, throwing me sideways against the panel. My feet went up in the air, my head banged against the side of the coach, and I had to brace myself to keep from sliding off the seat.

My companion must have been coiled for the moment. She sat still, with perfect balance, unmoved by the wild motion of our vehicle.

"Do you mean robbers?" she asked, but there was little interest in her tone.

"You're damn . . . ah, darned right I mean robbers. They rob this stage more often than not."

"I am prepared for trouble," she said. From a hidden pocket in her dress she pulled a Colt derringer, the small kind of .41-caliber pistol. This one had a pearl handle, like the ones women dealing faro sometimes carried.

I couldn't help it. I laughed aloud. "Honey," I said, "that peashooter won't stop any self-respectin' robber. He'll have it off you before you can blink. You best just keep it hidden." I was so curious about this child that I could burst, but I was also beginning to like her. There was a bravado about that small gun that someone like me couldn't help but admire.

She put the gun back in her pocket and turned her eyes out the window, clearly through talking to me. But there couldn't have been much for her to see—desert floor, cac-

tus, dry gulches, and in the distance, some purple mountains that gave the false hope that you might be headed
toward a better land. Alkali dust flew up around the
wheels of the stage, and seeped in through gaping holes
in the frame of the vehicle and around the doors and windows. Overhead, the sun beat down, and inside, the carriage was hot—really hot.

"Usually rob the stage at Contention," I said conver-
sationally. "Dry wash just this side of the tiny town. It'll
take us better'n two hours to get there."

"Is it always robbed?" she asked, and I thought I
caught a tremor in her voice. She began to twist the ring
on her finger.

"Not always," I said reassuringly. "Only once about
every five or six trips. And it was robbed trip before last.
I think we're okay."

There was another long silence.

"What you gonna do once you get to Tombstone?" I
asked. "I mean, you wealthy? If you got enough money
to support yourself, someone'll steal it from you. And if
you don't . . . well, there ain't but one kind of work for a
pretty girl like you. And somehow I don't think you're
that kind."

"I . . . I don't know what you mean," she said, and I
didn't know whether to believe her or not. "I can find
work in a restaurant or something," she said, but I could
tell she only half-believed it herself. She looked so vulnerable that she made me remember myself all those years
ago when I was young and innocent.

"I been on the line," I said boldly, "and I've run a
house. And I can tell you I'd hire you in a flash, but I
wouldn't be doin' you a favor. You'd be old in five years,
dead in ten."

It must have dawned on her what I meant, for her eyes
grew wide. "I won't do either thing," she said slowly. "I
have business in Tombstone . . . and I can provide for myself."

"Honey, I sure hope you're right, but somehow I have the feeling you need help."

Her chin went up in the air, though it was trembling slightly, and her eyes went out the window. Conversation was cut off. I tried to sleep and couldn't, because I kept glancing at her. She stared out that isinglass window at the great nothingness around us. We made it to Contention without incident, though I confess I was a little disappointed. I'd wanted to be able to say, "I told you so," and to—well, you know, "save" her by bullying the robbers. It was something I knew I was full capable of. After all, I only had to mention Doc Holliday's name and most folks in the territory would pale and go the other way.

It was a seventeen-hour trip, and I never could sleep on that blasted stage as it bounced and rocked over an excuse for a wagon road. We stopped at two roadside stations beyond Contention, and at each I clambered out to stretch my legs and exchange pleasantries with the driver and station man.

"You goin' back to that son of a bitch, Kate?" they'd ask, and when I'd nod, they'd say something like. "We'll get you a nice coffin one day."

"Comes to that," I replied, "you best be measuring him, not me. Doc don't scare me."

Even while I bantered with the stagecoach men, relieved myself behind a scrubby bush, and welcomed the chance to be out of that airless stagecoach, my traveling companion sat motionless inside through each stop. Even though she neither slept nor fidgeted, I figured she must have wanted to relieve herself and was afraid to venture out of the coach.

After the last stop, I did my usual ungraceful climb into the coach and ignored the catcall behind me. Heaving myself onto the seat, I said, "You got a name?"

She smiled. "As a matter of fact, it's Kate. Kate Farrell." There was that flicker of amusement in her eyes. "I thought it was strange we both had the same first name."

"Yeah, but you don't have the nickname . . . or the nose to go with it," I said. "Listen, Kate Farrell, you need anything in Tombstone, you tell somebody to find you Big Nose Kate. I got friends there—important friends." Well, Wyatt and Virgil were important—I just didn't have to add that I couldn't stand them and they hated me. Doc was the bond that held us all together.

"Thank you," she said simply. And then she asked a question. "Do you know Morris Tedley? I believe he's a banker."

I nearly hooted. Morris Tedley dealt faro at the Eagle Brewery. "A banker?" I asked incredulously.

"Yes," she said solemnly. "I believe with the Tombstone American Bank."

"There ain't no such bank in Tombstone," I said bluntly.

Her eyes widened again, this time in unwelcome surprise. "You must be mistaken. I've . . . we've had correspondence on that letterhead."

"Tedley must have a friend with a printing press," I said, "and there's only one in Tombstone. John Clum publishes the *Tombstone Daily Epitaph*. He could do up some fake letterhead."

She appeared to ponder this, though not without some unhappiness. Then, decisively, she said, "I'm quite sure he's a banker."

You can be "quite sure" if you want, I thought, but he ain't no banker in the sense you mean. Now I decided right then and there I was going to have to take this chicken under my wing if she was to survive. I didn't know what that low-life Morris Tedley meant to her, but I had my suspicions, and they had to do with that diamond on her finger. If he done her wrong, he deserved his come-uppance, and I was going to see that he got it. Kate Farrell was far too young and innocent be in Tombstone by herself, let alone figure out how to snare someone like Tedley.

"Now, Miss Kate Farrell," I said as the driver sawed on the reins to bring the horses to a screeching halt in front of the Dexter Livery and Feed Stable, "you go get yourself a room at the Cosmopolitan—it's the best place in town. You can eat there without goin' out on the streets, and you'll be safe. I'll come after you in the morning, and we'll find this Tedley fellow." Asleep in his bed after a long night gambling, I thought. Might not be a bad time to confront him. But first I had to find out what he'd done to her. I decided I'd deal with that in the morning.

"I appreciate your help," she said. "I . . . I was a little uncertain about what to do when I get here. The Cosmopolitan?"

"Right down Allen Street here, next block, as a matter of fact. I'll get someone to carry your bag down there."

Feeling like a foolish old mother hen, I watched as the driver hauled her bag off the top of the stagecoach. I hailed someone to help her with it, and threatened to tell Doc if he did anything but take it straight to the hotel. I gave him a silver piece, and then trailed them to the Cosmopolitan. Kate Farrell went in that door without turning around, like she never knew I was behind her. But she knew.

I found Doc at the Occidental Saloon, two doors down from the Cosmoplitan. It was the place Wyatt partly owned and where he and Doc and Morgan and Virgil spent all their time. Morgan was was the one I addressed.

"Morgan Earp, I got a job for you," I said.

"Already got one, Kate. Case you forgot, I'm the city marshal." He'd never liked me any better than I liked him.

"It's that Morris Tedley," I said. "You got to do somethin' about him."

"Morris Tedley?" Wyatt hooted. "He's a fly on the wall, couldn't cause any trouble if he tried."

"Well, he's tried, and he's done it. I don't exactly know what, but—"

Doc looked a little less drunk than usual, but the thing

about him was you could never tell by watching him just
how drunk he was. Now, he stared at me and drawled,
"Hello, Kate. Nice to see you back in Tombstone." He
was perched on a stool, and looked perilously close to
falling off it, even though his skinny legs were twisted
about the rungs. He gave me a lopsided grin, and I was
glad to see the old fool.

"Doc," I said, going over to him and almost whisper-
ing, "I'm glad to see you too. I really am."

He squeezed my hand, which was a real show of af-
fection for him. Morgan and Wyatt looked disgusted.

"Kate," Doc said slowly, "why the hell are you so up-
set about Morris the fly?"

So I let loose about Kate Farrell and how she was
looking for Morris Tedley and how she wouldn't tell me
what it was about and no young woman should be alone
in Tombstone and they had to do something, 'specially
Morgan, since he was the law.

"Sounds like a personal problem to me," Morgan said.
"I got rustlers to worry about, not broken hearts."

"Doc, you gonna' listen to this?" Wyatt asked impa-
tiently. "I'm goin' across the street to the Eagle and see
what's goin' on."

"And warn that snake Tedley," I snarled.

Wyatt just grinned, but Doc took my hand. "Let's go
home, Kate. I been missin' you, and you don't need to
bother your head about some girl that's foolish enough to
come this far chasin' a scoundrel. She'll get discouraged
and go back where she came from soon."

Back where she came from! It hit me I didn't know
where she'd come from. I tried to remember if her speech
gave away a place of upbringing, but she hadn't talked
much, and I couldn't place it.

Late in the night, when Doc lay snoring so loud I
thought he'd choke and die that way, I lay awake, tossing,
turning, wondering about Kate Farrell and her story. She
had become my responsibility, no matter how much Mor-

gan and Wyatt and Doc laughed and tried to discourage me.

Next morning, I was up early, before Doc even stirred. I dressed silently, pulling a clean but wrinkled shirtwaist out of my carpetbag, and putting on the same black broadcloth skirt. This morning, I did take some time with my "toilette," being much more careful than usual to secure the pins that held my hair in place and dabbing some cornstarch on my nose so that it didn't shine. I pinched my cheeks for color, and then gave that up and dabbed on a bit of the rouge I kept hidden from Doc.

Dressed the best I knew how, I went down Fifth Street to Allen and turned right to the Cosmopolitan Hotel. I told myself I was goin' for breakfast. While I was waiting for my flapjacks and sausage to appear, I went to the clerk at the desk. "Is Miss Farrell in?"

He bent his balding head over the register, and used his finger to follow name by name down the list, an irritatingly slow process. I stood there fuming, sure that my flapjacks were growing cold and hard. At length, the silly man raised his head, looked me directly in the eye, and said, "There ain't no Miss Farrell here."

"Impossible!" I stormed. "I followed her here to this hotel last night."

"You followed her?"

He seemed genuinely interested by this, and I considered bashing him across the face. Reason somehow prevailed. "Yes. I . . . I was concerned about her, and watched to be sure she made it safely to this place of retreat. Young girl, red hair, too innocent to be in a place like this." I looked around as though in disgust.

"This is the best hotel in Tombstone," he said indignantly. "But nobody named Farrell arrived last night."

"Did any woman alone come into this hotel last night?" I demanded, putting my face across his counter until that nose that made me famous was right up close to his own nose, which wasn't so small either.

He backed away a little, and then began again his
finger-following of names down the register. "Miss Waggoner!" he said triumphantly. "Miss Dorothy Waggoner.
She came in on the stage last night."

Now, I thought, we're getting somewhere. "What room
is she in?"

"Oh, I can't tell you that." He rolled his eyes heav-
enward and raised his hands, as though imploring the
Lord to help him.

The Lord had better help him, I thought, before I'm
through with him. "Either you tell me, or Marshal Earp
will be down here to find out if you been double-lettin'
rooms," I said.

It was, of course, the Earp name that threw terror in
his heart. "Room 136. Third door on the right, top of the
stairs."

Without even thanking him, I headed up the stairs. At
136, I knocked with loud determination, bound to find out
why this slip of a girl had lied to me about her name.

There was no response. I knocked again, louder, and
then shouted, "This is Kate Elder! You open this door and
tell me why the hell you lied to me!"

Still no response, until a drummer down the hall
opened his door and came to stand belligerently in the
hall. He obviously had had a hard night, for his eyes were
bleary, his hair stood on end, and he was totally unaware
that he was confronting me in his long underwear.

"Left early this morning," he said. "Quit the damn
racket."

Back downstairs, I berated the clerk. "Why didn't you
tell me she left early this morning?"

He shrugged. "I didn't see her leave. Haven't seen her
since she arrived. Maybe she don't want to talk to you."

I turned away in disgust and went to eat my breakfast.
The flapjacks were stiff and cold by now, but I ate them
anyway.

*   *   *

NOT MUCH SURPRISED Big Nose Kate Elder—she'd been around long enough to see it all—but she would have been astounded if she'd seen Kate Farrell—for that was her real name—leave her room at 5:30 in the morning— long before Big Nose Kate was awake, let alone thinking about the helpless girl she'd decided to take on as a cause.

Kate Farrell had darkened her red hair with boot black and tucked it under a beret. She wore baggy work pants held up by a rope belt, and a denim shirt that was too big for her and slightly frayed at the seams. Her worn boots were not cowboy boots like most men in the Arizona Territory wore, but the square-toed boots of the East. Her face bore blackened smudges, as though she had not washed for a day or more. Instead of going down the main stairs and past the desk, she ever so gently eased open the back door, clambered gracefully down the back stairs, and landed with a gentle jump in the alley behind the hotel. Then, with a quick look over her shoulder, she headed determinedly around the hotel to Allen Street and back to the livery, a woman—or young boy?—with a definite destination.

That destination was Dexter's Livery and Feed Stable. Body loose, walk confident, she strolled in to find the owner barely awake, rubbing his eyes and contemplating the day.

"You use someone to muck out the stables and harness horses?" she asked, pitching her voice so low that had Big Nose Kate heard her, she would have denied it was the same voice.

Sam Dexter looked startled. "Why you lookin' for a job so early in the morning?"

"I figure that's when people need help. You don't get goin' in the morning, you don't get goin' at all." The young person stood with arms akimbo, almost challenging the owner to hire him.

"What's your name?" he asked. "Where you from?"

"Name's Tom O'Toole. Where I'm from doesn't matter. I'm sixteen years old, and my folks are long ago and far away. I got to take care of myself." Well, it was only part a lie, Kate reasoned. She did have to take care of herself. And what better place to find out what was goin' on in town than a livery stable?

"You been around horses a lot?"

"All my life," came the reply.

Sam Dexter considered. "Let me see your hands," he demanded.

A pair of thin white hands were held out, but Dexter could see where calluses had been, the kind that came from holding reins. Big Nose Kate had never thought to look at the hands of her traveling companion. If she had, she'd have been even more puzzled.

"Been a while?" Dexter asked.

"Yes, sir," O'Toole replied. "I been on the road, catching rides where I can, walking when I can't. I . . . I want to stay one place for a while. And in town they tell me . . . well, they tell me you got a good reputation for taking care of horses. I like that." This last bit of flattery was delivered with disarming innocence.

Dexter nonetheless puffed with pride. "That I do, lad, and I'll not tolerate anything less than the best care of the horses entrusted to me."

"Yes, sir," came the reply.

"Pay's ten dollars a month and found."

"Don't need no found. I . . . I hooked up with somebody, and I got a place to stay. But I'll work whatever hours you want, however long."

Dexter considered for a long time, staring at this young boy, wondering if he was strong enough, had the endurance to muck out all the stalls, exercise the horses that didn't get ridden, keep the tack polished and shiny. "Okay, we'll give it a week," he said. "You can start now."

So Tom O'Toole spent the day hard at work. In each

stall, he stopped to stroke the horse's nose, talk to it gently, even affectionately. When he exercised the horses, he showed no fear even of the rank ones, and he rode with a confidence that Dexter had seen in few young men. He watched, seated with his feet propped on the desk, hat pulled over his eyes. But not much missed his gaze. He was satisfied he'd found himself a sure-enough gold mine of an employee.

When someone came for their horse, Dexter hollered out, "O'Toole, bring that bay from stall seven . . ." or whatever, and Tom O'Toole saddled and bridled the horse and led it forward. There was only one untoward incident in the day.

"O'Toole? Bring Tedley's horse from stall ten," Dexter called out. He was too far away to see the shaken look on his new employee's face, but soon the young boy came leading a skittish black Thoroughbred that pranced and offered twice to rear up on its hind legs.

Morris Tedley watched in digust. He was a medium-sized man, slender to the point of being dapper, with carefully pomaded hair and neatly creased nankeen trousers that, to anybody in Tombstone, identified him as a dandy. And he had an air of taking himself too importantly. "You there, boy! Can't you control that horse?"

The "boy" said nothing but, talking gently, tried to calm the horse, leading it slowly toward the front of the stable. Just in front of Tedley, the horse reared, lashing out with its front hooves. Tedley ducked and ran for cover, while Tom O'Toole hung onto the reins and finally calmed the animal.

When Tedley approached, he had his arm raised to cuff the errant stable boy.

Sam Dexter grabbed the upraised arm. "Now, I wouldn't be doin' that, Tedley. This boy done a fine job of calming that horse. Maybe you best see about training him yourself . . . or find another livery."

"There's not another livery in Tombstone," Tedley protested, his tone verging on a whine.

Dexter just nodded and walked away. Tedley threw a dirty look at the stable boy and roughly pulled his horse into the street, where he mounted with the awkwardness that showed his unfamiliarity with horses, and then slammed roweled spurs into the animal's side, making it take off in a great leap that nearly unseated the rider.

Watching, Tom O'Toole fervently wished that the horse had really bucked and thrown Tedley. The incident gave him an idea. "What kind of a man is he?" he asked Dexter.

Dexter shrugged. "Mean as sin, but there's no stuffin' to him. Poke him or threaten him, and he'll fall apart pretty fast."

Pondering this, Tom O'Toole went back to work.

At seven, Dexter said, "You best go on now, Tom. Been a long day. Don't want to wear you out the first day."

"Yes, sir. Horses are all settled for the night. You sure there's nothing else?"

"I'm sure. Be here at seven in the morning—five-thirty's a mite early for me."

Kate Farrell walked slowly back to the Cosmopolitan Hotel. She was tired, though she'd never have admitted to anyone else that it had been a long day. And her hands were raw with blisters—it had been too long since she'd held the reins of reluctant horses. And she'd never worked this hard from dawn to dusk.

At the Cosmopolitan, she once again entered by the back stairs. In the communal bath on the second floor of the hotel, she cleaned herself of the day's dirt, but left the boot black in her hair. Back in her room, she turned herself into a woman again, albeit a dark-headed one. She dressed carefully in a fresh broadcloth dress and again tucked her hair into a net—she didn't want that nosy clerk to notice the change from red to black. Then she sat at the tiny desk to write a note. Folding it into an envelope, she sealed it carefully and scrawled a name across the front. It was eight-thirty when she stopped in front of the clerk at the desk.

"Miss Waggoner?" the clerk said eagerly. "Did you have a good day. I mean, in your room all day . . ."

"I had a fine day, thank you," she answered serenely. And then: "Would you see that this is delivered by hand?" she asked, folding a dollar bill under the envelope so that he could see it.

"Yes, ma'am, Miss Waggoner" he said perfunctorily. And then he looked at the name. "You want to send something to Big Nose Kate Elder? Doc Holliday's woman?"

Dorothy Waggoner smiled blandly at him. "Yes, I do."

"She . . . she was here looking for you early this morning. I 'spect it was just too early for you to answer the knock."

"I imagine so," she said. Her manner was ladylike, almost slightly timid, and you'd never have known how she'd spent the day.

"Big Nose Kate Elder," he said, wrinkling his own nose a bit with distaste. "It don't seem like you'd have anything to do with the likes of her."

"Is that so?" Miss Waggoner said blandly, and sailed into the dining room.

Had the clerk been able to read the note he held burning in his hand, he would have known it said simply, "Can you come to my room at the Cosmopolitan Hotel, Room 136, tomorrow night at eight? With appreciation, Kate Farrell."

Dorothy Waggoner ordered pheasant for dinner. She found it well prepared and of good flavor. Shortly after finishing her meal, she retired to her room. Seven o'clock, she knew, would come early.

I ABOUT LEAPED out of my shoes when some no-good yahoo handed me that message.

"Clerk at the Cosmopolitan paid me to deliver this," he said, and disappeared as quick as the words were out of his mouth.

We were at the Occidental, and Doc was drunker than a skunk—belligerent drunk. "What the hell's that?" he demanded. "You gettin' mail by special delivery?

"None of your business," I replied, turning my back on him to open the envelope.

Wyatt and Morgan stared at me, their expressions half amusement and half distaste. I swear, if I'd had a gun I might've shot them both right then, thinking I was a no-good whore like they did.

My back turned to all of them, I smoothed out the note and read it. To me, it was a real puzzle. There was no Kate Farrell registered at the Cosmopolitan, and yet here I was invited—practically commanded—to appear there to see her the next night. Of course, there was no way in hell that I wasn't goin' to be there.

The next day, when I was filled with anticipation anyway, was a day that Doc chose to turn ugly. "No-good whore," he yelled at me. "Just waitin' around for me to hit it big in the mines."

Since he never worked the mines, I thought this was kind of funny, and I made the mistake of laughing.

He hit me broadside across the face with the flat of his hand, and I spun backward into the door frame. Within ten minutes, I could feel my eye begin to swell up. Doc, meantime, collapsed on the bed and began to snore.

Wonderful, I thought. I'll go see Kate Farrell with a black eye.

When I got ready to leave that night, Doc was still angry. As I started out the door, one skinny but strong arm blocked the doorway, and I was forced to stop. "It's that woman after Morris Tedley, isn't it? I'm tellin' you, Kate, you stay out of that. Whatever business she has with Tedley, she can handle herself. I don't want to have to be beggin' Morgan to look out for you."

"I can look out for myself," I said angrily.

I appeared at Kate Farrell's room right on the dot of eight—breezing by that dumb desk clerk without so much as a "How d'ye do?"

She answered my knock immediately, and the door opened to admit me to a room tinier than I thought it would be. Kate Farrell wore a calico wrapper and looked like somebody's kid sister. She didn't look like someone mixed up in two identities and heaven knows what else— except that her gorgeous red hair was now sort of a dingy black and looked like it needed washing.

Before I could blurt out my questions, she said with a small gasp of sympathy, "Kate! What happened to your eye?"

"Walked into a door," I said. "Just wasn't watching." What I wasn't watching close enough was Doc's hand coming toward me.

She shook her head, and I knew she wouldn't have understood about Doc punching on me. In the world she came from, men didn't hit women.

"How come you registered as Dorothy Waggoner?" I asked bluntly, ready for the truth to be out. "And why is your hair black?"

She laughed lightly, "I don't want Morris Tedley to recognize me," she said. "I was sure you guessed that."

"He did you wrong, didn't he?"

She considered for a long minute. "Do you promise not to tell anyone?"

"Cross my heart," I said, and made the appropriate gesture. I was about to jump out of my skin with curiosity. I lived in a world where men did women wrong, but not the kind of wrong she was talking about.

"He . . . he took money from. . . ." Her eyes watered up, and she could hardly get the words out. She paused a minute, seemed to get control of herself, and said, "He took money from my father to go into business in Tombstone. We were to be married once he'd made a success of himself."

That no-good scoundrel, I thought. Hangin's too good for him. "Where's your father? And why'd he trust that lowlife?"

"Father's in Ohio—that's where I was raised, and where Morris grew up. We've known each other all our lives. He was always churchgoing, respectable . . . I just can't believe he's not a banker here, like he told Father. I had to come see for myself . . . and maybe try to get the money back."

"Your father let you come this far alone?" I asked suspiciously.

"He thinks I'm visiting an aunt in Kansas. By the time he finds out I'm not, I hope I'll be back home."

"So what's your plan?" I asked, my mind whirling with ways this poor thing might get her money back from Tedley. "You'll get it back," I said confidently. "He's nothing more than a fly on the wall."

"Fly on the wall?" she echoed.

"Yeah, that's what the Earps call him. They say he ain't got no stuffin', ain't no more of a threat than a fly on the wall."

"The Earps?" she asked.

"Earps are three brothers recently come to Tombstone. Morgan's the marshal, and Wyatt owns a gambling house, and Virgil . . . well, he's just here. They spend a lot of time with . . . my friend, Doc Holliday."

She wasn't interested in any of them at the moment. "I don't know what to do, but I'll have to get that money back for Father. It was all he had in the world, and he's . . . well, he's getting on in years." She dabbed at her eyes.

"Well," I said, "you could always try to beat him at faro."

"Faro?" she asked, clearly puzzled.

"Card game. With a board. Banker—that's Tedley—

draws two cards at a time, and players put bets on the board against what the banker draws."

"I . . . I don't think I could learn to beat him at that. I suppose by now"—she let out a small sob—"he's learned to be very good at that."

"Only medium," I said, "from what I heard. But I doubt you could count on beating him. Might cost you more than you make. You got to watch to make sure the dealer's honest about where he takes the cards from . . . and I doubt that's the case with Tedley, that fly on the wall." I proceeded to tell her everything I'd learned from Doc 'bout faro, and she took it all in wide-eyed.

"I can't risk money like that," she said, shaking her head. "I'll have to figure some other way to get Father's money back from Morris. The marshal you mentioned. Would he help?"

I shook my head. "The Earps don't get involved with what they call 'domestic matters.' They're too busy gettin' rustlers and the like, building themselves a big reputation." My bitterness showed in my voice.

Kate Farrell was clearly disturbed. She put one hand up to brush her hair away from her face, and that's when I saw it. She had blisters on her hands, raw, weeping blisters that must have hurt like hell.

"What've you done to your hands?" I demanded.

She looked at them ruefully. "A little honest work, that's all. They'll toughen. I've . . . I've had blisters like this before."

"Only thing I know that would cause blisters like that is a pair of reins," I said, waiting for her to tell me something that would answer some of my questions.

She smiled. "You're too smart for me, Kate Elder. You promise not to tell?"

I nodded. "I already made that promise once," I reminded her, "and Big Nose Kate keeps her word."

"I'm sure," she said hastily, not wanting to offend me. "I got a job at the stables, disguised as a boy named Tom

O'Toole. I . . . well, I've always known horses, been around them. Father trained horses. It was his business until . . ." Her voice choked, and then she recovered. "Until his health failed." She looked down at her hands. "Working at the livery seemed better than being a . . . what do you call them? . . . a biscuit-shooter?"

Now how she knew that word for a waitress, I never would figure out. I was dumbfounded by this girl.

IT WAS NEAR ten o'clock when I left the Cosmopolitan, past the hour when a respectable woman should be on the street alone, but that never bothered me. I went two doors down to the Occidental in search of Doc—and secretly hoping Morgan would be around.

They were all there, even Virgil this time. All three Earp brothers greeted me with nods and expressions that were almost sneers, but I was used to it and paid them no mind. Doc said, "Lo, here cometh the lovely Kate."

"Stop that foolishness," I said, batting his hand away from my waist. "Order me a whiskey."

"Say 'Please,' " Morgan said, and I gave him what I thought was a withering look. I'd heard a lot about withering looks and never known what they were.

"Is there a new stable boy down to the livery?" I asked as casually as I could.

"Now, Kate, why would that matter to you?" Doc asked, frowning at me.

"Just heard a rumor. Always feel bad when a young boy hits town—they're running toward what they think is glamor, and it's more often disaster."

"Didn't know you were so softhearted," Morgan said. "Yeah, there's a new lad down there. Nice kid, name of Tom O'Toole. Works hard, knows horses, and can take care of them."

And she's ruinin' her hands, I thought.

* * *

THE NEXT NIGHT, long about eight o'clock, I said to Doc, "I believe I'll go on to the Eagle."

"Goin' to play faro?" he asked suspiciously.

"I might," I said. "I just might. You gonna give me any money?"

He snorted in disgust and forked over twenty-five dollars.

"I won't get rich on this," I said, "but I'll try."

It was just as I thought: Kate Farrell, disguised as this Waggoner woman with dark hair, was at the Crystal Palace. This time she'd added a pair of wire-rim spectacles to her disguise, and the dress she wore was pale blue with a bit of lace at the neck. It made her look—well, virginal—but of course she was! Now a new woman, unknown in Tombstone and unescorted, usually drew a lot of attention at a place like the Eagle, but Kate looked so young and innocent that nobody paid her any mind after looking once at her in surprise, as though wondering what a girl like that was doing there. She drifted from blackjack table to roulette to faro, apparently fascinated by each game. But at the faro table where Morris Tedley was dealing, she lingered, slightly back of the players.

Tedley looked up. "Want to play, ma'am?" His voice was oozing with charm and he had that seductive look that dealers use to lure people into their games. He sure didn't recognize her, though I was holdin' my breath.

She shook her head to indicate no, and then seemed to change her mind. "I . . . I've never played," she said in a sweet young voice. "Will you tell me what to do?"

Tedley knew opportunity when he saw it. "I certainly will, young lady," he said. "Just sit right down there. Now you place your bet on this board, and when I take two cards from the bank here . . ."

Kate appeared to be listening to him as intently as she had listened to me the night before. Something told me Morris Tedley's run of good luck might have just run out.

I dodged behind people and pillars and kept Kate from seeing me. I didn't figure it would help our relationship for me to be caught spying on her, but that was what I was doing. And I watched in amazement as she cleaned Tedley out.

Each time she'd win, she'd say, "Ooh, is that money mine?" like a little kid who'd just been given a piece of candy.

"Yes, it is," Tedley said smoothly, raking it toward her.

Now I knew he was playing that old game of letting the beginner win until he was hooked—only this time it was a she—and then taking him for all he was worth. I was in a terrible quandary—interfering with gambling was strictly against the code of behavior in Tombstone, but how could I watch this poor girl lose whatever she had?

I eased up behind her and put my hand on her shoulder.

She turned, looked up at me, and her face lighted. "Why, Kate, you're my guardian angel. I'll win if you stay by me."

Tedley looked at me with clear disgust. "You don't be coaching her now, Big Nose Kate."

"Me?" I asked innocently.

I tried to slip her Doc's twenty-five dollars, but she pushed it away.

There came a point when it was suddenly clear to me that Tedley had lost control. The pigeon he thought he was working was really winning. I watched the sweat gather on his forehead, watched carefully as he shuffled the cards—and had to remind him sharply once, "From the top, Tedley, not the bottom." He threw me a dirty look.

An hour later, Kate Farrell was ooohing and aaahing over the five hundred dollars she'd won. "I can't imagine all that's mine," she said. "I best be going now."

Tedley was desperate. "It's . . . it's usually not done to leave with that much of the house money," he said.

He must have been thinking, *What the hell! She's young and green, and I can bluff her*.

Kate gave him her sweetest smile. "Well, I'll come back another night, and I'm sure you'll take it all back from me."

"That a promise?" he demanded.

"Surely," she replied. Then: "Kate, will you walk back to the hotel with me?"

"You bet I will," I said roughly, throwing Tedley one of my withering looks. "You need protection." Once we were in the street, I demanded, "How did you do that? You never played before!"

"Why, Kate, I just listened to everything you told me, and it certainly worked. I'd . . . I'd like to give you some of this money."

"No," I said roughly, "I don't need it. Is that . . . does that satisfy Tedley's debt to your father?"

She laughed merrily. "Oh, my, no. Not anywhere close. But it's a start. I'll put it in the safe at the hotel."

"Ought to put it in the safe at Morgan Earp's office," I told her.

"The hotel will be fine," she said serenely. "And thank you for walking back here with me." She said good night and disappeared through the doors.

I stood outside, dumbfounded. Somehow, there was something about this story I wasn't getting.

I DIDN'T SEE Kate Farrell for several days, not until I began to hear about what she'd done.

At first I was too busy with troubles of my own to worry about that sweet little girl. Things were heating up between the so-called rustlers—the McLaury brothers, Johnny Behan, and Ike Clanton—and the Earps, and Doc was right in the middle of it. Some said he knew about this murder and that, and it was said that Ike Clanton was gunning for Doc.

Now, having a man gunning for him never made Doc

nervous. As I said, and I may repeat myself, Doc wasn't afraid of dying since that what he was doin' anyway. And a bullet would be a lot faster and neater than coughin' himself to death. But havin' a man call him a liar made Doc frantic . . . and he took his frantic out on me. I had another black eye, and I told him I was tired of bein' hit.

There's folks to this day will tell you Doc and I split because I got . . . what's the word? abusive? yeah, that's it. But that ain't the truth. Doc got abusive, real bad so.

Anyway, in the midst of this, we're in the Occidental one night, and Wyatt says to me, "Your friend Tedley's having a run of bad luck. I heard he lost a bundle the other night."

"Yeah," I muttered, "I heard too." I wasn't about to tell him I'd been there and what I saw.

"Now his horse pitched him ten miles out in the desert. Broke his leg, and he lay there half a day 'fore anyone found him. Sorry fool is lucky he didn't die."

His horse pitched him? The horse he stabled at the livery? Something else was strange here. My mind spun with possibilities, none of them good.

"He dealin' with a broken leg?" I asked.

Wyatt aimed for the spittoon. "Naw, the doc's got him laid up in traction. Can't deal for two months or something. He'll lose a lot of money." He chuckled, to show that Tedley's loss of money meant nothin' to him.

I took myself down to the Dexter's livery that very day, and told Sam Dexter I wanted to see his new stable hand. "O'Toole," I said, triumphantly pulling the name from my memory. "That's it. The O'Toole boy."

"Now, Kate, what business you got with him?" he asked.

"Don't you be bothering me, Sam Dexter. Just call that boy."

He hollered to the back of the stable, and pretty soon a young boy in baggy clothes and a kind of beret hat came runnin' up between the stalls.

"Lady"—did I hear Dexter hesitate over that word?— "wants to talk to you," he said, jerking his head in my direction.

"You be sure I do," I said, approaching the "stable boy" with menace.

"Yes, ma'am?" he said, all innocence. "What can I do for you?"

I didn't even recognize her voice. This was a soft voice, but that of a young boy not a girl, and there was a difference to the words—I couldn't put my finger on it, but I figured Kate Farrell was as good an actress as she was a gambler.

I looked at Sam Dexter, with his ears all perked. "Not here," I said. "Come out on the street."

Allen Street was crowded with people coming and going, talking, shouting, all involved in their own business. Nobody paid us any mind, except to shove by us. I pulled "Tom" east toward Chinatown, where nobody would for sure bother us.

"You do somethin' to spook Tedley's horse?" I asked bluntly.

He looked directly at me. "No, ma'am, Miss Kate. I . . . I never would do that. I heard what happened, and I'm just surprised it didn't happen sooner." Wide, innocent eyes looked directly at me. "That horse was too much for him to begin with."

"You didn't put a burr under the saddle so that it would be all right at first, and then finally work its way into that horse's hide?" I knew the tricks, you see.

He gave me an amazed look. "A burr? Why would I do such a thing? Course I'm sorry Mr. Tedley's hurt. But Kate Farrell, she wouldn't be sorry at all." And with that, he said, "I have to get back to work now. Nice to see you, Miss Elder." And he was gone.

I didn't even tell Doc about the encounter.

I forgot about Morris Tedley, and even Kate Farrell, a few days later when Doc got mean drunk and told me to

pack my bags and get out. "Go live in that tent whorehouse of yours," he said. "It's where you belong."

My Irish—well, all right, it was Hungarian—was up,
and I warned him. "You throw me out, you old fool, I'll
tell Sheriff Behan you were one of the four that held up
that stage outside Contention two weeks ago."

He yawned. "Go ahead and tell 'em," he said. "Nobody'll believe a drunk like you."

"Drunk?" I exploded. "Who's the drunk? You'll see,
Doc, I'll get you in trouble."

Well, I did just that. Swore out an affadavit that Doc
had been in on that robbery. Probably that was the dumb-
est thing I've ever done in a long career of being dumb.
Next thing you know, there was a warrant out for Doc's
arrest. That made me sober up—well, I mean, sober up
in my thinking. I never was drunk! Trouble was, Morgan
and Wyatt were pushing me to leave town.

"If I leave town," I said, assuming my haughtiest voice,
"I can't tell them I was wrong about Doc being involved."

Morgan's voice was tight. "You'll tell them that and
then you'll leave town."

"I'll tell them that," I said, "and then I'll decide what
I want to do."

"You leave town," he said in a straight tone, "or your
tent whorehouse is likely to burn just like Morris Tedley's
tent."

I was astounded. "Morris Tedley's tent burned?"

"Yeah, the one he lived in. Yesterday afternoon. He's
lyin' there with a broken leg, and the thing catches fire.
No one knows how. Only reason he didn't go up in flames
with it was that stable boy you was asking about, he walks
by and pulls Tedley out of the flames. Close call." Earp
shook his head, though there wasn't much sympathy on
his face.

Kate Farrell had set fire to Morris Tedley's tent! I wondered if she'd stolen his money first, and I made myself
a promise to go to the Cosmopolitan that night.

"Where's Tedley now?" I asked.

"Got him a room at the Cosmopolitan. He screamed he couldn't afford it, but wasn't much else to do." Earp shrugged.

"I'll sign your new affadavit," I said. "I got other business to see to." Both of them at the Cosmopolitan, I thought. Morgan didn't even know what trouble could happen. But I was beginning to suspect.

"You're gettin' on the afternoon stage," Morgan said with real menace in his voice. "I don't care about that 'other' business." He grabbed my arm. "I'm goin' with you to Doc's while you pack, and then I'm escorting you to the stage."

"You can't run me outta town!" I yelled indignantly, jerking my arm to pull it loose. Morgan held firm, and next thing I knew I was being marched down Allen Street at a good clip—away from the livery and the Cosmopolitan both.

With Morgan standing over me, I threw some clothes in a carpetbag. Took everything I had at Doc's. "What about the stuff I got at my place? And who's gonna run my place?"

"I'll find someone to buy you out, and I'll send your stuff to Tucson. You ain't comin' back to Tombstone, Kate."

"Don't you go bettin' too soon," I said under my breath. The real reason I was lettin' Morgan do all this— even though I was fightin' and complainin'—was that I was ready to get away from Doc, and I knew right then he would take Morgan's side against me. In a week, he'd be begging me to come back to Tombstone.

But what would happen to Kate Farrell/Dorothy Waggoner/Tom O'Toole in a week? Better yet, what would happen to Morris Tedley?

MORGAN LITERALLY SHOVED me into the stage, even before I could hoist my skirts out of way. I was about to

turn and give him a good slap when I saw the other passenger in the coach.

Kate Farrell herself! Red hair and proper brown traveling outfit. She smiled complacently at me.

"You!" I said. "Did you finish your . . . uh . . . business
with Morris Tedley."

She smiled, and there was no pretense of innocence
about her any more. "Yes, I did, thank you. Quite satis-
factorily."

I paid no mind as Morgan slammed the door shut—
almost on my foot—and the stage lurched forward. "Who
are you?" I asked.

She shrugged. "It's only fair you know. I am Kate Farrell, and I am from Ohio . . . but by way of some other
places. Morris Tedley and I, we were partners . . . we ran
games in St. Louis, Kansas City, finally Tucson. But he
double-crossed me." Her eyes turned steely when she said
that, and I wondered how stupid I could have been ever
to think of her as innocent. Clearly, she was more so-
phisticated than I would ever be . . . and more clever.

"I had to reclaim the money he stole from me," she
said. "And I decided to make his life difficult while I did
it. He won't try anything like that on me again."

Little did I know how seriously she meant that!

We rode in silence. There wasn't nothin' I could say
to her. I sure as hell wasn't one to pass judgment on one
of my fellow sisters. After all, hadn't I just gotten revenge
on Doc in a pretty unfair way, accusing him of robbing a
stage? And yet . . . there was something so calculating, so
cold about the Kate Farrell who now sat opposite me.

I recalled that when we rode in, I was the big mouth,
telling her all about how it was in the Wild West. Now I
was quiet, silenced by her cleverness and her . . . what was
the word I wanted? Something to do with the devil.

Once again, she never set foot out of the stage, never
had to relieve herself or eat the greasy food at the stops,
never slept. I did all of those things . . . otherwise seven-

teen hours on a stage would have driven me crazy. Or, as
Doc would have said, crazier than I already was.

As we pulled into Tucson, I managed to stammer,
"Well, I wish you luck, Miss Kate Farrell. Doesn't seem
to me, though, you need my good wishes. You make your
own luck."

She took my hand and looked me straight in the face—
only this time, those eyes weren't so innocent. "I'm sorry
I tricked you. You were a good friend, and I took advantage. I don't usually do that to friends."

I had just one question for her. "How old are you?"

"Twenty-eight," she said without flickering an eye.

"You fooled me," I said as I jumped down from the
stage. The driver threw down my carpetbag and I headed
off to find lodgings, without ever looking back to see
where Kate Farrell went or if she went alone.

JUST AS I'D said, Doc wrote within a week, begging me
to come back, saying the business about the affadavit was
all cleared up, and no one suspected him any more of
anything except bein' a drunken fool—some admission
from him!

I took the stage back one more time—not knowing it
would be my last trip to Tombstone. No one met me, and
I hefted my bag to Doc's by myself. He was really glad
to see me, the old coot! It sort of pleased me.

But then he said, "Let's go to the Occidental and cel-
ebrate your homecoming."

"Morgan'll just tell me I have to leave town," I said.
"Let's just stay here."

"I don't have a bottle. We're going to the Occidental."
That was how quick his mood could turn.

So we went to the Occidental, and there was Morgan
and Wyatt and Virgil.

"Hey, Kate," Morgan said, "that girl on the stage with
you. Who was she?"

"Name's Kate Farrell," I said, and wondered if I should go into all her aliases.

"You know," Morgan said slowly, "I done some investigatin'. But you already knew she was that new stable boy, and she was that dark-haired young woman at the Cosmopolitan."

I didn't say anything.

Morgan went on. "In one disguise or another, she seemed connected to everything bad that happened to Morris Tedley. And the day he dies, she leaves town."

"Tedley's dead?" I said.

"Yeah. I'm calling it suicide. Couldn't take losin' his money, breakin' his leg, and all that. Man reaches the breaking point pretty quick out here. Shot himself."

"What caliber gun?" I asked

"Why? It was a .41," he said.

I was tempted to tell him, "That wasn't no suicide." But I kept my peace. Sisters under the skin had to stick together. And I knew without asking that Morris Tedley had died penniless.

Killer in the Dark

∽◦◦∽

by Ed Gorman

Ed Gorman is a Midwesterner, born in Iowa in 1941, growing up in Minneapolis, Minnesota; Marion, Iowa; and finally settling down in Cedar Rapids, Iowa. While primarily a suspense novelist, he has written half a dozen Western novels and published a collection of Western stories. His novel *Wolf Moon* was a Spur nominee for Best Paperback Original. About his Western novels, *Publishers Weekly* said, "Gorman writes Westerns for grown-ups," which the author says he took as a high compliment, and was indeed his goal in writing his books.

TUESDAY 4:03 P.M.

THE TALL MAN in the dark city-cut suit says nothing. He is not unfriendly.

That is to say, he smiles when the others smile; he gives approving nods when the others do likewise. He picks up one of the ladies' magazines when it is jostled to the floor of the stagecoach. He even offers a stick match to one of the men who wants to light his cigar. But he does not join in any of the conversations. He seems distracted. He stares out the window. Every time one of the passengers mentions Tombstone, which lies just ahead, his dark eyes flicker.

4:09 P.M.

"I don't want to piss you off, Virgil."

"Well, it sure as hell isn't going to do me any good if you lie to me, Sam. So tell me, what did the council say?"

"It wasn't the whole council."

"No?"

"It was just three out of four."

"That's a pretty good number."

"It don't matter what they said, Virgil. I shouldn't ought've brought it up in the first place."

When you were city marshal of a town as wild and dangerous as Tombstone, you needed loyalty from your deputies. The trouble with Sam Purcell was he took loyalty too far. From time to time he'd hear things that Virgil ought to know. But he wouldn't share them because he was afraid he'd hurt Virgil's feelings.

But he'd made a mistake.

He'd started telling Mal Bottoms, one of the other deputies, what he'd overheard at the town council meeting this afternoon. And Virgil had happened to be within ear distance.

So now Virg and Sam stood in the empty outer office with all the wanted posters and the smell of burnt coffee and Virg's Scottish pipe tobacco, and Virg said, "Tell me, Sam. And tell me right now."

Sam sighed. Sam was a champion sigher. In fact, Sam was far more articulate with his shoulders than he'd ever been with his tongue.

"Well, in a nutshell what they said was, and you know I sure as hell don't agree with it, was that maybe you were the right kind of town marshal for when a bunch of cowhands want to come in town and raise hell, but maybe you're not the right kind of town marshal for a manhunt."

"Meaning Bobby Gregg."

"Meaning Bobby Gregg. They said he's probably in Mexico by now."

"Not unless he has wings. Suzie Proctor was murdered less than thirty-six hours ago."

"Like I said, Virgil, it ain't me sayin this, it's the council."

"Three out of four."

"What the hell do they know anyway?"

"That all they said?"

"Pretty much."

Virg smiled. "Meaning there's somethin you left out."

"Well."

Now it was Virg's turn to sigh. He wasn't as good at it as Sam, but he gave it a good try. "I'm supposed to be lookin for a killer, Sam. I believe—despite what the town council says—that he's hiding right here in Tombstone. Now I need you to tell me what else the council said and then I need to get back to work."

Sam made a face. "They said if Bobby Gregg gets away—Suzie bein' so popular and all—that they'll take your badge away whether Wyatt Earp's your brother or not."

"They said that, did they?"

"I didn't want to tell you, Virgil. But you made me."

"It's all right, Sam."

"You pissed off?"

"Not at you."

"I'm sorry, Virgil."

"I know you are, Sam. Now let's get back to work."

A few minutes later, strapping on his Colt and grabbing a Winchester, Virg Earp left the town marshal's office. He had three different posses looking for Bobby in the areas surrounding Tombstone. He kept on working the town itself. A lot of people smirked when he passed by. A few even made jokes about him. Mostly that he was too lazy to go out into the blistering desert sun and look for Bobby.

Nobody but Virg seemed to believe that Bobby was hiding somewhere in town here.

5:01 P.M.

He was an unlikely killer, Richard Turney. He ran one of
Tombstone's three newspapers. He'd been educated in the
east at Rutgers, and had seriously considered attending
Harvard Divinity School afterward. He would have made
a fine parson. But he decided he could be more effective
as a journalist. He worked for a time for the *New York
Daily* and the *Chicago Gazette*. He was the champion of
the miners and their families and a favorite of the area's
ministers, priests, and one rabbi. Too many newspaper
editors were in the pockets of the rich and powerful. Not
Turney. His office had been raided, trashed, burned. He
had been followed, threatened, shot. His wife Jean Anne
had been assaulted and very nearly raped. And yet he kept
on being the spokesman for the poor, the weak, the sick,
the mentally troubled, the Irish, Jews, colored, Chinese—
and for decent working conditions in the mines, where
men died every single day of the week and usually un-
necessarily.

He hadn't wanted his affair with Suzie Proctor to become any more than friendship. And yet—taking on a life
of its own—it had. He had a lovely wife and two lovely
children. And most of all, he had his reputation for rec-
titude. Let other Tombstonians carry on as if they lived
in a whorehouse . . . but not Richard Turney.

But what use was a fallen sinner to his community . . .
or to himself? He'd tried to convince her to quit her job
as his assistant, and quit sneaking off with him in the
evenings. She was officially engaged to Bobby Gregg,
who was a fine young man. Did she want to destroy her
future with him? But she was adamant. She loved Richard. There was nobody else for her. Bobby was a child.
Richard was a grown and wonderful man. A wonderful
man who'd strangled her.

He'd crept home late, from dragging the body to the
river. Jean Anne had been awake when he came in. De-

manded to know what had happened. Listened in shock and terror as he'd told her all of it. A parson's daughter whose good looks—it was said—were utterly wasted on so religious a woman, she'd told Richard he must not confess. Because if he did, who would defend the poor and powerless of this area?

He got up several times during the night. Couldn't sleep. Wanted to go to the town marshal's office and confess. She awoke each time with him. Wouldn't let him go.

Walking the streets now was difficult for him. He wanted the forgiveness of every citizen, for he felt that his behavior—first his adultery, then the killing—surely required their understanding.

How could he live with this, even though suspicion had naturally fallen on Bobby Gregg, who had been seen arguing violently with Suzie three hours before the murder?

5:07 P.M.

The stranger was the last person off the stage. He stood in the dusty twilight looking around the legendary town with icy interest.

Boomtowns usually deserved their reputations. But men like the Earps—hired guns who wore badges—took care to see that such towns were safe for those who had to live there. You could whore it up and drink it up and gamble it up if you stayed in the places that the Earps owned. But anywhere else, they'd run you in fast. And your fine would help swell the town treasury, to which they were entitled to a goodly share.

He began to walk, a cheroot stuck in one corner of his mouth. With his dark suit, dark flat-brimmed hat, and dark-handled .44 riding in a dark leather holster, the stranger brought a funereal aspect to a part of town where most folks were dressed for partying. His younger brother had walked these same streets for the past few years after settling in here as a miner. The kid had kind of drifted around before. The stranger had been so happy to hear he'd taken a regular job, he'd bought the kid a whole bunch of new duds including boots, and put twenty-five Yankee dollars in an envelope too. He'd sent them to the kid for his twenty-first birthday.

He continued to walk, to watch. He did not walk unnoticed.

SAM, THE DEPUTY, took note of him when he walked down Main Street and stopped in at the telegraph office; Mal, the other daytime deputy, took note of him when he left and walked over to the Bountiful Hotel.

Sam went over to the telegraph operator and asked to see what message the stranger had sent.

Burt Knowles, the telegrapher, laughed. "He was foxin' ya, Sam. He wanted to see if anybody was followin' him. He just come in here and stood over in the corner smokin' that cheroot, and then he left. Then he got down to that corner where Mal picked him up, and he stood there and watched you come in here."

This was greatly amusing to Burt. Much less so Sam.

THE STRANGER REGISTERED at the hotel and went directly to his room. He slid off his clothes except for his underwear, and then climbed into bed and started reading a book by Sir Walter Scott.

He decided he'd get a little reading done before the local law came to call.

The knock came thirty-five minutes later. The stranger recognized the man in the door immediately. Virgil Earp.

"I come in?" Virgil said.

"I wouldn't be foolish enough to stop you."

Virgil nodded and entered. "Just doing my job, mister. My responsibility to know who's in town and what their business is."

"Yes, I've always heard that Tombstone only lets the elite stay within its city limits."

Earp gave him a sharp look. "Nobody's claimin' we're angels here. But there's different kinds of bad men. Bad and real bad. The real bad ones we don't let in. Now, I'd like to see some identification if you don't mind."

The stranger, who was wearing his suit again, slipped a hand inside his suit jacket and pulled out a wallet. He handed it to Earp.

Earp looked through it and whistled. "You're a Pinkerton?"

"That's right."

"And your name is Ben Gregg?"

"Right again."

"You any relation to Bobby?"

"I'm his older brother."

"You know he's wanted for murder?"

"He didn't do it."

"How do you know?"

"I know Bobby. He's emotional, but he's not a killer."

Earp handed the wallet back. "I don't suppose you might be a wee bit prejudiced."

"He's my brother. I spent twelve years with him on an Ohio farm. I know how he reacts to things. He told me all about Suzie. How she'd agreed to marry him, and then backed out all of a sudden. And how he was going crazy."

"You saw him?"

"He wrote me."

"He must be quite the writer."

"He finished the tenth grade. He's a smart kid."

"He's also a killer, Mr. Gregg. I don't take any pleasure saying that to you. I really don't. I have brothers too, and I know what this must be like for you. The best thing you can do is help us find him. And then have him give himself up before somebody decides to play hero and shoots him—or a bunch of drunks get together and try to lynch him."

"He didn't kill her."

Earp walked back to the door. "I wish you'd help us, Mr. Gregg. You might save his life."

"Save his life until the territory can hang him, you mean."

"I don't make the laws. I just enforce them."

"Noble sentiment."

Earp opened the door, lingered. "You seem like a smart man, Mr. Gregg. It's hard to be objective in a situation like this. He's your own flesh and blood. You might think you're helping him—but maybe you're really hurting him. And yourself in the process. There are laws against aiding and abetting a fleeing felon, Mr. Gregg." He paused. "Even when the felon happens to be your brother."

Then he was gone.

6:03 P.M.

"How come Daddy is in bed?" twelve-year-old Ruth asked Jean Anne Turney. She seemed older than her calendar age, having the poise and elegance of her mother.

"He's not feeling well, honey."

"How come he doesn't feel well?" Nicholas Turney said. He was eight.

"He just has a little touch of something is all, sweetheart." She was a lovely, elegant woman—even in a much-washed and much-patched cotton pinafore she was elegant—with the features of classical statuary and eyes that sparkled with life. Until you studied them anyway. Some folks claimed to see a hint of madness there—all that religion she so deeply believed and espoused. Most pioneer stock had brought their religion with them. But they weren't about to let themselves become fanatics about it. Leave that to the Mormons.

"What's a 'touch' mean?" Nicholas wanted to know.

Jean Anne smiled at him. "Correct me if I'm wrong,

but didn't we sit down here to have supper?"

He giggled. He loved it when Mommy played school-teacher. It was fun. "We sat down to eat. E-A-T."

"Correct," Jean Anne said. "Now, can you tell me *why* we're not eating?"

He giggled again. "Because we're gabbin'. G-A-B-B-I-N."

"That's right. Gabbing. You can't put food in your mouth while you're yapping." Jean Anne smiled. "I thought we were going to quit gabbing—*and* yapping—and eat our dinner."

Corn on the cob; potatoes; green beans. All from the garden Jean Anne tended to so devoutly.

"But first, let's say grace."

Jean Anne usually concentrated on each and every word of every prayer she said. Sometimes people just rushed through prayers, mumbling the words and letting their minds stray to other matters. What was the point of praying then? God wanted total attention. God wanted utter and uncorrupted devotion.

But tonight, as the children raggedly prayed their way through grace—she loved the sound of their small earnest voices; and surely God too must be pleased when He heard such pure and innocent voices—tonight she was no better than the mumblers she castigated.

She couldn't think of anybody but Richard; of anything but Suzie Proctor's death.

Forgive me O Lord, she thought. But I can't have this scourge brought down upon my children. If people know that their father killed her—accidentally or not—then they'll be marked for the rest of their lives, like a version of Cain's mark.

She tried not to think of her proper folks back East, her father a parson so respected that the Episcopal bishop declared him the finest church orator he'd ever heard. The scandal—adultery, death—would surely hasten his death. He had a bad heart and was already failing.

She had never told a serious lie in her life; and the few small lies she'd told she'd later admitted to, and asked the person's forgiveness.

But she knew this was one lie she would have to be part of for the sake of the children. Bobby Gregg was the man the mob was looking for. Bobby Gregg was the man who would have to stand trial for Suzie's death. She tried to convince herself she was doing the only thing she could. Bobby was single, had no roots, would probably not live long anyway, given his temper. He and Richard were good friends, pitching horseshoes whenever they had a chance, Bobby eating dinner here a couple of times a month. And Bobby was a good young man, but—but Richard, on the other hand, was the father of two, a successful businessman, and a man who brought the truth to all. She knew as a Christian that all lives were important . . . but (and forgive me, O Lord, if this is the sin of pride) aren't some lives more important than others in the scheme of things?

"My beans are cold," Ruth said.

"Gosh, I wonder why," Jean Anne said.

"Because we were yappin'," Ruth said, and looked at Nicholas.

"Huh-uh. We were gabbin', not yappin'," Nicholas said.

"It's the same thing," Ruth said.

"Huh-uh," Nicholas said. "Is it, Mommy?"

Are some lives more important in the vast scheme of things? Jean Anne knew she was treading on some mighty dangerous territory here. Playing God was what she was doing. Making decisions only the Good Lord Himself should be making.

But how could you look at these two wonderful children and not spare them the mark that would be associated with what their father had done?

But Bobby Gregg . . .

7:23 P.M.

Serena's brother Tom made ninety dollars a month as a bricklayer. Serena, all of seventeen, made $150 on average. Serena was a prostitute. Not that Tom knew. He lived in Denver. Not that her mama knew. Though she lived in the house with Serena, she was still suffering the effects of her stroke. She was not yet forty-five, but looked eighty, crabbed up in her wooden wheelchair. Sometimes she shit herself. Sometimes she talked in that slow, retarded way to phantoms and ghosts. And sometimes she sang this strange, melancholy, beautiful song in the clear, dear voice of the young woman she'd once been.

Serena worked right in Tombstone. There was one house that had been particularly good to her, so she'd pretty much stayed there. But she always came home. She worked four hours a night, and then went back to her mama's place for the night. She had a face and figure that could command so much money for so little work. Every man who came into Mama Gilda's wanted Serena. And who could blame them?

Tonight Serena was late for work. There'd be a battle with Mama Gilda. She'd begun to wonder if Gilda knew what was going on, with Bobby Gregg and all. Serena, who was in love with him, and had been since the very first time she'd ever seen him, had hidden him in the attic ever since they'd found Suzie Proctor's body. She believed Bobby—even if few others did—that he hadn't killed Suzie. And she knew damned well that if Virg Earp (who had visited her more than a few times at Mama Gilda's) ever found Bobby, he'd do what he needed to to satisfy the public at election time. He'd made a big show against it—but he'd let a lynching take place. And he wouldn't indict anybody after it either.

Serena's mama had had a bad time just around dusk. She'd started throwing up and talking crazy. She'd also started running a hell of a fever. Serena—knowing that

Doc Wright would just say to let the fever run its course—
had spent nearly two hours with Mama before getting the
old lady in bed and settled down for the night.

Now, a dinner of squash, peas, wheat bread, and apple
pie filling a large plate, she climbed the stairs to the attic.
She had the sensation of climbing into night itself. Except
for a tiny window in the front of the house, no light lib-
erated the attic. It was a prison of darkness.

She heard Bobby start as she reached the narrow square
where the ladder ended. She heard him draw his six-gun.
Bobby was scared, no doubt about it.

She walked slowly through the gloom, over to the
small window where Bobby sat propped against the wall.
She'd brought him a chamber pot a few days ago. The
pot was starting to reek. When she had time later tonight,
she'd empty it for him.

"You hear anything today?" he said. Then: "I really
appreciate you doing this for me." He sounded so young,
frightened. He'd told her at least a dozen times about a
lynching he'd seen up to the Missouri border one time.
How the man had screamed and sobbed until the noose
finally broke his neck.

She couldn't see much of him, but the moonlight
hinted at the strong lines of his face and the vulnerable
beauty of his brown eyes. He was all man, Bobby was.

"The manhunt's still on if that's what you mean."

"What's Virg sayin' about me?"

"He still thinks you're in town."

"They still laughin' at him?"

"Sure. Most people think you're long gone." Then:
"You better eat, Bobby."

She liked to watch and listen to him eat. He ate vulgar,
jamming the food into his mouth without pause, and
smacking his lips loudly and pleasurably. All this evoked
a maternal feeling in her. That was it. He was her lover,
but somehow he was her brother, too.

"They're gonna get me, aren't they?"

"Not if you stay here. I can protect you, Bobby."

She wouldn't mind spending the rest of her life like this. Someday, they'd give it up and wouldn't hunt for him anymore. And by that time, he'd be so grateful that he'd never leave. That was *her* fear. That he would run off. And so she did everything she could to convince him that he would certainly be lynched if he ever left this house.

"You just stay here. I'm going to see your brother to-night."

"My brother! He's here?"

"I wired him, Bobby. I figured you'd want me to."

"Good Lord, if anybody can figure a way out of this, it's him."

"I have to be careful about seein' him, though. Virg Earp is probably watchin him pretty close."

"My brother," Bobby marveled. "My brother!" He sounded as if all his troubles had been swept away. He pulled her to him and kissed her. It wasn't the passionate, open-mouthed kind of kiss she wanted from him. It was more just a chaste brother-sister kiss right to the left of her mouth. But it would have to do for now. Bobby didn't love her yet. But by the time this whole thing was over and the real killer had been found, he'd be so grateful that he'd never leave her. Or, if the killer was never found, she'd keep right on hiding him, as she'd thought of earlier.

"I got to go now, Bobby."

"You tell him it's all up to him."

"I will, Bobby."

"You tell him they'd just love to lynch me."

The initial enthusiasm was waning. He was beginning to understand that Pinkerton man or not, his brother maybe couldn't stop the manhunt from taking its inevitable course.

"You just finish your supper and rest, Bobby."

"Sometimes I hear your ma down there singing to her-self."

"It's pretty, isn't it?"

"Yeah, except it's sort of spooky too. And I don't mean that to give offense."

"I know what you mean. All the time I was growin' up, she called it her ghost song. That's sort of what it's like."

"Ghost song," Bobby said. "That's a good name for it all right."

6:43 P.M.

Ben knew about conducting a murder investigation. He'd spent an hour where they'd found the young woman's body. He got down on his hands and knees with a mag-nifying glass and went over everything he could that looked even vaguely useful. He found a variety of buttons, the butts of cigars and cigarettes, small scraps of paper, tiny pieces of broken bottle glass, and numerous other bits and scraps that he dropped into a plain white envelope. Virgil Earp apparently hadn't found any of this material interesting. Ben Gregg had had the advantage of training under Alan Pinkerton. Alan was much taken with the way Scotland Yard and its French counterpart used the idea of a "crime scene" in homicide. You staked out a wide area of ground where the body had been found, and then you carefully combed it for anything you could find. You never knew what would prove helpful to your investiga-tors or the police or the district attorney. So you kept everything and cataloged it.

From time to time, he thought of something else too. According to the newspaper account, she'd been stran-gled. But then a heavy object had been used to smash in the side of her skull. It seemed an odd combination. If the killer had strangled her, wouldn't that be enough? Why then smash a rock against the side of her head?

Finished with his work, he went back to town and spent two hours talking to people who knew Bobby. None of them thought he was the killer. It was hard to know why they were saying this. Did they really believe it, or were they just saying it to make an older brother feel better? He learned nothing special from these interviews, except that Bobby's best friend in town was probably an "upstart" editor named Richard Turney. Turney was, in the parlance of many, a 'goody-goody,' but as one saloon enthusiast said in his smiley, slurry voice, "Them two, yer brother and that fuckin' big-mouth newspaperman, they're just about the two best horseshoe players in the whole territory. They get more people t'watchin them than them shimmy dancers do when they come here with the county fair every summer."

Turney's name was the only one that was repeated, which was why Ben Gregg was on his way to the Turney house right now.

He might find some answers there.

7:03 P.M.

The young ladies at Mama Gilda's glared at Serena when she came into the parlor. The three men in the room could feel their anger, and wondered what was going on. Then they saw Serena and didn't *care* what was going on. This beautiful, small, delicate creature with the exotic eyes and erotic mouth was the one they wanted. Their first choice anyway. Maybe that's what the other girls were so mad about. That they weren't as pretty or erotic as Serena.

Mama Gilda, a tiny woman with a big temper, pushed her way into the room and said, "I want to see you, young lady, and right now."

The other young ladies smirked with delight. Mama Gilda was finally going to give it to Serena. And it was way past time.

7:04 P.M.

Mike Craig's leg wasn't getting any better. It'd been broken in a landslide and then gangrene had set in somehow.
Word was, he was going to lose it. Which meant he
couldn't serve as Virg's chief deputy no more.

Virg hadn't decided on who Mike's successor would
be. In truth, it would be hard to replace Mike. He was a
redheaded Irishman who knew how to keep his temper
and how to walk away from a whiskey bottle. The townspeople liked him and the deputies liked him. Hell, some
of the prisoners in the lockup liked him. Mike had a mil-
lion stories.

Sam Purcell meant to have the first deputy's job. He'd
served three years with Virgil now, and had learned a
damned good lot about being a good, sober public server.

He probably didn't have any real edge. Virg might well
not choose him, in fact, which was why Sam was hiding
behind the tree across the street from Serena's house on
the edge of town.

As usual, Sam had paid a visit to Mama Gilda's Tuesday afternoon. He always collected Virg's share of the
money Mama kicked back to him. That's when he'd overheard two of the girls running Serena down. Who does
she think she is? She gets paid too much already, and
now she isn't even showing up regularly? Sam asked
Mama Gilda about this, and the madam acknowledged
that Serena had indeed begun acting strangely lately. She
works so few hours as it is, Mama Gilda said, and now
the little bitch don't even show up for *them* half the time.
She didn't have no idea why Serena had suddenly stopped
showing up on time. Far as Mama Gilda knew, nothin'
bad had happened, not there anyway. No man had mis-
treated her, none of the gals had stolen from her or beat
her up, and she got her money full and on time just like
always.

Which had given Sam his idea. Though not a lot of

people knew it, Serena and Billy spent their free time together. Good Christian boy like Billy, he didn't want nobody to know, of course. What kinda upstandin' young man keeps company with a whore? It was one thing to visit her at Mama Gilda's and pay for it; but it's another thing entirely to keep *company* with a whore.

So tonight, he sees Serena coming late to Mama Gilda's and he remembers what them gals was chewin' on the other day, how Serena's been comin' into work late and not doin' like she ought to in general. Not like her, Mama Gilda had said, shakin' her head; not like her t'all.

Well, what could a young gal have gone and got herself all caught up in? Could be a rich man; could be some kind of venereal disease even a whore was embarrassed about; or it could be . . . hiding a fugitive.

What if Bobby was in her house somewheres?

Well, that's what Sam was doing here. Just ten, fifteen more minutes and the sun would start sinking, and he'd be sneaking across the road.

If he brought in Bobby Gregg, he'd be first deputy for sure.

7:10 P.M.

Stupid bastard.

Thinks Bobby doesn't see him.

Well, of *course* Bobby sees him. And sees him good too.

Saw him come up from the ravine and go hide behind the tree. He think Bobby's blind or what?

The thing now is, what's he gonna do next? Bobby wonders.

Is Sam gonna charge the house and shout for him to come out?

Or is he gonna try and sneak inside and real quiet-like check out every room in the house?

Bobby'd put money on sneaking inside. Sam fancies himself a real foxy type. Fought in the war with a buncha farm boys and been sailin' bullshit stories about it ever since. Hear him tell it, Union Army didn't fear nobody as much as they did him.

Then Bobby feels unholy. He is a churchgoer, Bobby, and he has been praying his ass off ever since the manhunt started. He prays and prays and prays, and he feels holy and safe and good. And then he spoils it all by thinking bad thoughts about people and how much he dislikes them and thinks he's better than them and would like to do them harm, and then he doesn't feel holy anymore. He chased holiness away, and now he's just one more miserable desert rat.

No.

He takes it back.

I hope you come in here, Sam, and you don't find me, and you go back home to that Mex wife and kids of yours and you have yourself a real nice, real long life.

That's what's in my heart, Lord. It purely is.

But then he hears Sam on the back porch, sneaking in. Only way he could make any *more* noise was if he fell down into a buncha pots and pans.

Subtle, he ain't.

Then he hears the back door itself squawk open. Door swelled and doesn't fit frame right anymore.

He's inside, Sam is.

Searching.

Only a matter of time till he finds the attic.

O Lord, please keep Sam from finding me. Please, Lord. Please.

IT STILL HURT where Mama Gilda slapped her. Serena sat on the bed in her room, touching her fingers tenderly to the sore spot on her gracefully carved cheek. Bitch probably put a bruise there.

The place was crowded tonight. Lots of whiskey, lots of laughter, lots of prairie flowers fading fast. That was her biggest fear. That somehow she'd wake up one morning and look like them. And it happened so fast sometimes. Take young Helen from Pennsylvania. Came West with her folks, who got killed in a sudden flood. Ended up working as a whore so she could support her two little brothers. Mama Gilda was good to her. Serena had to say that for the old bitch. Mama Gilda saw to it that the kids were put in school, that they found a nice little cabin to live in, and that Helen was home most nights before ten o'clock to tuck the boys in.

But wasn't nothin' Mama Gilda could do about Helen's looks. Year ago, Helen had been almost as beautiful as Serena. Fresh, young, and vital. A lot of her johns—especially the young cowhands—fell in love with her and asked her for her picture and things like that. But as with many of the girls, disease aged them fast. Bad luck of the draw, to be sure; but this bad luck seemed to come to so many of the girls. First, Helen had come down with just crabs, then with gonorrhea. And she was always catching colds and having influenza and getting the chills and then the fevers for no reason—not even the doctor—could see. And it had all taken its toll. Pale, tired, drab, she had worked her way down toward the bottom of popularity. No men, either young nor old, asked for her anymore, and Mama Gilda had begun to give her day work—helping clean and sew and do bookkeeping work (at least Helen had a bit of education and was smart, which was more than you could say for most of the other girls), the sort of jobs girls got if they were diagnosed with syphilis, Mama not allowing no girls with syphilis to cavort with her customers till the doctor said they couldn't infect nobody.

So far tonight, Serena had had two of her regulars, and they'd both said that she seemed in sort of an owly mood. She'd put on her best smile and forced herself to laugh a lot, but they knew better and she knew better. She'd worked them hard too, so they'd come faster.

She needed to be alone to think about Bobby. Now

that she was away from the house, she saw how foolish she'd been. Somebody was bound to find him there. People were always coming over to drop things off for her mother. One of them was bound to see or hear something.

Why couldn't Virg Earp just find the real killer anyway?

She knew what that posse would do if they ever did find Bobby. All his nightmares about being lynched would come true.

At this point, his brother was his only hope. That's probably why she was so anxious. She needed to get out of here and go see his brother.

But the clock hands didn't seem to move. She was sure they hadn't moved in an hour.

A knock.

"It's me, Princess. Tom Peters."

"Hi, Tom."

"Are ya decent?"

"No, I'm not."

"Then I'll be right in."

It was the same joke he used every time he came to Mama Gilda's, and usually the idiocy of it made her smile despite herself. But not tonight.

She hurried to the mirror. She took pride in her job. She fixed her hair from the last tumble on the bed, freshened her makeup, daubed on some more perfume.

If only helping Bobby was this easy.

But she had to help him before the lynch mob did.

7:36 P.M.

It made for a lonely portrait, the sight of Gregg the Pinkerton man in his shirtsleeves bent over a table where he'd spread out everything he'd found where the girl had been strangled, a flickering lamp his only companion. He was a city man and this was a nowhere town, and in his occasional sighs you could hear the pain that time had inflicted on him, and that he had sometimes inflicted upon himself.

The wife and two sons who had left him when it became clear that he would never give up this detective business and stay home like a real father. The illegitimate son he'd fathered a few years later, who'd smothered to death in his crib one night. The earnest if desperate attempt to reconcile with his wife—traveling by train mid-winter for six hundred miles—only to see her sitting in a restaurant with the man she intended to marry, the man he suspected she loved more than she'd ever loved *him.* Self-pity, self-hatred, a lonesomeness that was a physical ache sometimes—these were the detective's lot, redeemed only by his sense of humor about himself. Nobody could make better jokes about him than he could. And—for everybody's sake—he made such jokes often.

Thank God for detective work. It almost made up for the loneliness. It almost made him forget all the terrible mistakes he'd made in his personal life, not least of which was being such a miserable absent father to his boys. He never would've said that out loud, of course, about detective work being his one true love. Might end up in an asylum if you said it loud enough. Hey, ain't that the guy who said he was in love with detective work? And there he'd be in one of those padded rooms where they slid your food in through a little flap in the bottom of the door. Don't want to get *too* close to the crazy man. Whatever he's got might be catching.

But he lived for the British magazines that detailed all the exciting new work being done in England and France. Fingerprinting was just coming into its own. No court had yet allowed it to be used as evidence, but that was only a matter of time. Phrenology—determining a person's criminal inclinations by the shape of his head—was fading in popularity, and that in itself was exciting. He'd always considered it useless. Scotland Yard was also beginning to create a file on every criminal they arrested.

This might be the most important development of all, and Gregg was pleased to see that Alan Pinkerton—despite the reluctance of city cops to do it—was likewise creating his own files on criminals he apprehended.

The two items that interested him most now were a black button that appeared to have come from a dress jacket and two different boot heel prints. The ground there was clay and showed up prints pretty well. He'd gotten down on his knees and scratched a pencil over a thin piece of white paper. The designs on the boot heels showed clearly. There was one other heel design. A much smaller one. A woman's shoe. The heel had been worn down, but you could still see a faint V on it.

He went back to the button. It was the size of a cuff button on a suit jacket. While black was a reasonably popular color with men—easiest to dust off and clean—there were very few men who wore the color regularly. It was considered too hot for summer, for one thing. And too dour for any kind of festive occasion. He started making a list of men who wore black regularly. Preachers, mortuary men, town officials who had to go to a lot of funerals, and carriage-trade types who might get invited out to a fancy dance every once in a while. He could eliminate the latter as a category around here. There *weren't* any fancy dances. He could also eliminate town officials. Folks around here understood how hot it was. They didn't expect anybody to dress in black at functions.

But why would a preacher or a mortuary man be out where a young woman was killed?

He opened himself a pint of rye and pondered. Sometimes, pondering was a whole lot of fun.

8:07 P.M.

Nicholas said, "She's cryin' and she won't stop."

"Your sister?" Jean Anne said. And then realized that was one of those stupid little things people said without thinking. Who *else* would be crying but Ruth? "Where is she?"

"On the swing."

"You finish drying those dishes for Mama. I'll be right back."

"It's *her* turn to dry."

"Don't sass me now; don't you sass me, you understand?"

Nicholas was old enough, and savvy enough, to understand when his mommy was real serious about her threats. Sometimes she was just sorta half-serious and you could tell by her tone of voice that she didn't really want to do anything to you. But then there were times—as now—when he knew that strap wasn't far away if he didn't do *exactly* as she told him.

He took the dish towel down and started drying the dishes.

Jean Anne could hear her before she reached her. Crying bitterly into the last cool traces of daylight.

"Quit swinging, honey, I want to talk to you."

"I don't want to talk, Mama." And kept right on swinging, pigtails flying, the hem of her dress fluttering in the slight wind. She spoke through tears.

Jean Anne grabbed the swing. "What's the matter with you? Don't you do what your mama tells you to do?"

She had to grab the swing even harder to bring it to a full stop. A few times Ruth scuffed her shoes in the worn earth of the swing's path, slowing the swing even more.

"Now I want you to tell me why you're crying."

"I just think Gus is sick is all."

Gus was their sad-faced hound. He was older than Ruth. Jean Anne could see her daughter was lying. She said, concerned now because Ruth so rarely lied, "I need to know the truth. I can't be a good mama if I don't know the truth. You don't want the Lord to punish me for bein' a bad mama, do you?"

Ruth didn't say anything for a time, and then she lifted

her sweet little face and looked at her mama. "I guess I just get scared sometimes. Like right before a storm."

Ruth was given to odd moods, moods that sometimes worried both her parents deeply. She did indeed get scared before storms; the smell, the suddenly brooding sky, the sharp decline in heat—she frequently hid under the bed. She was so grown-up in many ways—people often mistook her for sixteen or thereabouts—but there were still strong elements of the little girl in her too.

Ruth was silent. Cows, horses, a distant coyote, nightbirds; the restive and restful sounds of a farm as night fell.

"Honey, what are you tryin to say?"

But Ruth, fighting back another round of tears, wouldn't listen. She jumped from her swing and took off running toward the pasture.

Leaving Jean Anne to wonder—what in the Lord's name had *that* been all about?

Nicholas came out the back door. "I'm done with the dishes, Ma. Will you draw pitchers with me later?"

"Yes," Jean Anne said. "Yes, I will."

Nicholas went back inside. He was such a good little boy, uncomplicated.

She wondered what was wrong with Ruth.

8:10 P.M.

He was starting to sweat, Sam was. He'd felt all right entering the house, but once inside, his balls started to shrink and his stomach started to knot and his asshole started to get tight and his breath started to come fast and ragged and the sweat started to pour off him. He felt like some Mex working the fields at high noon. That kind of greasy, filthy sweat.

The downstairs was empty. He'd gone through it room by room. Nothing. Dinner smelled good, though. For a whore, Serena knew how to run a house real good. Trouble was, by the time she was ready to settle down—all rotten-toothed and disease-scabbed like a leper—who the hell would want her? Who would want to stick his dick into a honey pot that had been fouled by so many other dicks? No man with any sense; no man with any pride. No man Sam knew.

He had a piece of peach pie. Sitting right there just like he'd been invited, a nice little vase of flowers on the table and everything. And he was eating.

Now wasn't that the damndest thing you ever heard of?

This is a man who reads all the dime novels. Who has a very glorified ideal of what a deputy should think, do, and be.

And so what does the sonofabuck do when he sneaks into a house after a cold-blooded mad-dog killer?

He sits his wide ass down on a kitchen chair and helps hisself to a piece of pie. Peach pie. He would've preferred punkin (his word for pumpkin), but this is better'n nothin', that's for sure.

And it doesn't end there.

Because he eats another piece.

Serena's probably gonna wonder what the hell happened to her pie. Her ma is upstairs crippled. She sure as hell didn't come down here and get any. And (if Sam's hunch is right) Bobby Gregg is hiding in the attic, and *he* sure wouldn't've snuck down here either. For a piece of pussy, yes, maybe so. But not for no piece of pie.

But that's where Sam's wrong.

Because Bobby got to wondering upstairs what ole Sam was doin' downstairs. You sneak into a house, you check it out room by room, how long can it take you? Five-ten minutes at most. And that's if you're checkin' under the bed and in the closets and all that stuff.

And Sam's been in the house here a good twenty minutes. So what the hell's he up to?

No sense in waiting to find out.

No sense waiting up here liked a treed fox just waiting for the inevitable.

He's gonna surprise the sonofabitch.

Has to be very quiet. Can't put the attic ladder down. Too much noise. All he can do is take off his boots and hang from the open hatch, and drop to the floor in his socks and hope to hell Sam doesn't hear him.

But Sam is too busy eating to hear him. You can't shovel that much pie into your mouth without at least a little bit of it gettin' in your ears.

So here sits Sam shovelin' pie into his face.

And here comes Bobby sneakin' up on him in his socks.

And there squats this huge black fly on the last slice of pie left, and Sam reaches out to brush it away when he accidentally hits the slender vase and knocks it over on the table.

Except—

The spilled water in the vase runs backward because the table isn't level—runs right over the edge of the table and right on his crotch, and he's wearing these gray work pants and the soaking water make it looks like he pissed his pants.

And then—

There's this six-shooter pressing against the back of his head—

And Bobby says, "You just put your gun on the table, Sam, so I can see it real plain."

"Look at me, Bobby!" Sam says. "People're gonna say I wet my pants I was so scared of you. You kill me here, that's just what they'll say for sure! Then all the time my kids're growin up, their fuck-face little friends'll say your old man was so scared a Bobby Gregg he pissed his pants!"

"Just calm down!"

"This ain't no way for a man t'die, Bobby!"

"Dammit, Sam, I'm not going to kill you."

"You're not?"

"No, I'm not."

"Well, you killed Suzie Proctor."

"No, I didn't."

"You didn't?"

"No."

"Then who did?"

"You're the lawman. You tell me."

"You didn't kill her, why you holdin' gun on me?"

"Because I'm gonna escape. Because if I stay here you'll take me in."

"I got to, Bobby. It's my job."

"Well, you'd be takin' in the wrong man."

"Don't tell nobody, all right?"

"Tell 'em what?"

"You know, about me eatin' the pie and all."

Bobby grinned. "Eatin' pie and havin' wet pants. Guess that wouldn't make you look real good, would it?"

"My kids'd get teased somethin' awful."

"I think you're worried a little more about yourself than your kids."

"So what if I am?"

"I'll make you a deal, Sam."

"What kind of deal?"

"You give me a half-hour head start, and I won't tell nobody about the pie."

"Or my pants?"

"Or your pants."

"Nobody?"

"Nobody. Not a single soul."

"I really am jus' thinkin' of my kids, Bobby."

"Guess I'll have to take your word for it, won't I?"

"You really didn't kill her?"

"I really didn't kill her."

Sam looked at the table. "So I sit here half an hour?"

"Yep. You don't holler for help and you don't go into town."

"There's a piece left."

"I see that."

"What if I ate that last piece?"

"I'll tell you what, Sam."

"What?"

"You don't holler and you don't run into town for half an hour, and I'll tell Serena I ate the whole pie myself."

"Ya will?"

"I will."

"The whole thing?"

"The whole thing."

"You think she'll believe ya?"

"Sure she will." Then: "That last piece looks mighty good, doesn't it?"

Sam smiled. "Now that you mention it, it sure does."

8:07 P.M.

Ben Gregg knew it was late to go calling, but he hadn't gotten around to talking to the Turney family. Maybe they could be helpful. Several people had mentioned that Bobby was a good friend of the family.

He passed down the streets of saloons and gambling parlors. There had been a time when such noises had been exciting to him. No arms had seemed warmer than those of a whore; no drink more nourishing than whiskey. But these things and his wanderings as a Pinkerton had cost him the only woman he'd ever loved, and his children. The detective's way of life was legitimate; the other things weren't. And now they offered him only bitter reminders of how foolish and young and empty he'd been.

A faint light pressed at the window next to Turney's front door. Townspeople went to bed later than farmers. Maybe he wouldn't be waking anybody up.

He knocked.

He looked around him at the hills. On the other side of them was the river where the young woman's body had

been found. It came down to two things: Bobby needed
an alibi, which he apparently didn't have; or Ben, or
somebody, had to find the killer fast.

The man in the door had an Eastern quality that gave
his grave but handsome face a real dignity. The wide forehead, dark, wary eyes, brooding brow, long nose, and wry
mouth bespoke both intelligence and humility, not a combination you saw very often. People with brains flaunted
them like young girls with their first bloom of breasts.

"Gosh, I thought I was seeing things," Turney said.
"You look like your brother so much."

"Only older. Bobby doesn't have any gray in his hair
yet. At least not the last time I saw him."

"Not yet he doesn't."

Ben put his hand out and the men shook.

Turney said, "Why don't you come inside. There's still
some of the day's coffee left."

"That sounds good. Thank you."

As soon as he was inside, he saw a very pretty girl of
twelve or maybe older staring at him from behind a blue
curtain that no doubt hid a bedroom. She looked sadder
than anyone her age ever should. He sensed she wanted
to say something to him. She opened her mouth a few
times tentatively. But no words came out.

The coffee was good. Jean Anne, a very good-looking
woman, served it, and then she sat down with the men.

"I just hope Bobby gives himself up before they find
him," she said.

"Then you're assuming he killed her?" Ben said. He
didn't make it an accusation—as if she was betraying
him—he just asked her a question.

"I, well, I—" Despite his gentle tone, his question had
clearly rattled her. Then he noticed that her eyes had met
those of the girl who was peeking out from behind the
curtain. They shared some kind of secret.

"All she's saying, Ben," Turney said, "is that guilty or

not, he has to avoid being caught by one of those posses. They'll lynch him for sure."

"Do you think he's guilty?" Ben asked.

Turney too looked flustered. "This isn't easy for us."

"He's our best friend," Jean Anne said, wiping floury hands on the front of her pinafore.

"He has supper with us two or three or three times a week," Turney said.

"And we sure don't think he *did* do it," Jean Anne said. "Not deep down anyway. Even despite the way things look."

Ben was troubled by their unease. Why should they be so nervous answering questions as straightforward as his? He wasn't trying to trick them or trap them. He was just trying to find out about his brother. But they were firing glances back and forth and tapping their fingers on the table and constantly shifting in their chairs. Alan Pinkerton drilled into the heads of his operatives certain telltale signs to watch for during interrogations. The Turneys were displaying them all.

"He was here the night of the murder," Jean Anne said.

"Oh? How was he acting?"

They glanced at each other again.

"He was pretty down," Turney said. "The Porter girl had told him she didn't want to marry him."

"He told you that?"

"Why, yes," Turney said. "I was at the office working on some papers. He'd been here with Jean Anne and told her all about it. Then when I got home, he told me all about it too. He was pretty drunk by then, though."

"He drink a lot?"

"Not much actually. And we don't keep anything on hand here in the way of liquor."

"But he was drinking here?"

Turney said, "He'd brought his own bottle of whiskey."

"Did he make any threatening remarks that night about the Porter girl?"

Another exchange of glances. Jean Anne shook her head. "Not really. I mean, it was obvious how hurt and angry he was. But no threats—or at least I can't remember any." She looked at her husband as she said this.

"I can't remember any threats either," Turney said.

"About what time did he leave?"

"Oh—" She nodded at her husband. "Do you remember?"

"I wasn't paying much attention, I guess."

"Just a guess."

"Maybe ten."

"Ten. And was he still drunk?"

Jean Anne shrugged. "Not as much, I think. I'd given him some coffee."

"Was he still talking about the Proctor girl?"

"Oh, no." Turney smiled for the first time. "By then, we were on the subject of politics."

"I see." Then: "So you were here the whole time?"

"Why, yes," Turney said, sounding surprised. Here they'd been talking about the evening, them relating how Bobby had been acting all evening, then all of a sudden Ben Gregg seemed to be questioning if Turney had even *been* here. "Why would you ask that?"

"Somebody thought they saw you about nine o'clock."

"Well, if they did, it was somebody who was peeking through my window."

"Who said that anyway?" Jean Anne said. She was angry.

"It doesn't matter. You said you were home."

"And you believe me then?"

"If it's the truth I believe it."

"I don't like the tone of that, Mr. Gregg," Jean Anne said. "We love your brother. He's like one of our own family. We're trying very hard to believe he's innocent. But we have to tell the truth. We have to say exactly what

happened that night. You wouldn't want us to lie, would
you?"

"No, I wouldn't."

"Well, there you have it then. *My* husband was home
the entire night. If someone said they saw him anywhere
else, they're wrong. And Bobby acted just the way we
said he did. He was a lot soberer by the time he left and
he'd quit talking about the Proctor girl."

He saw her again, the girl. Peeking out from behind
the curtain. Again, and for a reason he couldn't explain,
he felt that the girl wanted to say something to him. He
wondered what. He was intrigued.

This time, her mother saw her too. "You get back in
there and get to sleep, young lady."

She vanished.

"She likes to listen to adults," her father said. "She has
a lot of curiosity."

Jean Anne smiled fondly. "She has my husband's
mind. My son and I are bright enough, I suppose—but
Richard and Ruth are the real brains in the family."

"Oh, now," Turney said. But he said it in such a way
that Ben knew they'd had this particular little joust many
times.

"So Bobby left and that was the last you saw of him?"

"Yes."

"And you haven't had any word from him since?"

"No."

Ben looked around the area by the front door. Turney's
Wellington boots stood there. The Easterner had made no
concession to the styles of the West. Given his
Edwardian-cut clothes and his boots, he would have been
right in fashion in downtown Boston. It was the first sign
of vanity he'd seen in the anxious man.

Ben stood up. Walked to the window. "Right over that
hill is the river where the body was found? You see anybody on the hill that night?"

Without looking at each other, they both shook their heads.

"Virgil Earp asked us about that," Turney said. "But we couldn't be much help to him there either."

"Didn't hear anything either, I suppose? Screams, anything like that?"

"Nothing, Mr. Gregg." Turney cleared his throat. "Nothing at all, I'm afraid."

Ben turned back from the window and as he did so, he made sure to knock his foot against one of Turney's Wellington boots. He bent down to right the boot, and in doing so took a close look at the heel. A V symbol was raised on the heel, the V for Victor Boots. It matched one of the heel patterns he'd traced on the muddy bank.

Turney said, "My wife bought me those for my last birthday."

"You've got a good eye for boots, Mrs. Turney."

"Thanks. I wanted to get something that would last."

"Well," Ben said, "I guess I'll be going. I've still got some work to do tonight." He didn't know if he had his killer. But he did know that he had somebody who'd been there that night.

Just as he was turning to the door again, he saw the girl—Ruth—watching him from behind. He'd never seen a girl so forlorn. She looked as if she'd been crying too. But it must have been silent crying, otherwise he would have heard her. As in most frontier houses, the rooms were very near each other.

"We're praying for Bobby," Jean Anne said.

"Night and day," said Turney.

"This may turn out all right," she said. "Sometimes the Lord surprises us."

"Yes," Ben said, "sometimes he does."

He opened the door. The night was cool. He wanted to be out in it. It promised a kind of clarity that would help him escape all the complicated lies he'd been treated to here.

Ruth was still watching him.

He said good night again and left.

8:47 P.M.

Bobby aches when he sees the lights of town. So many
pleasures a man takes for granted in normal times. Just
the liberty of walking free and unfettered down the street.
Or the pleasure of sipping a friendly beer in a saloon. Or
watching town girls in their town dresses walk coyly past
him.

It is a different world now that he is being hunted. At
any moment somebody could step up and arrest him. Or
open fire on him. The way the town hates him, nobody's
going to complain if he gets shot in the back.

The alley is narrow and dark. He crouches behind a
tree. Sweat stings his eyes. He smells rank from his time
in the attic. He wants to reach the mouth of the alley
across the street. That will bring him to a straight path to
Richard Turney's house. Richard and Jean Anne are sensible people. And his best friends. They'll loan him
money. Help him escape from town. That's all that's left
him now. Escape.

He leans away from the tree. Looks down the street.
All the houses dark or darkening now that bedtime nears.
Another pleasure a free man takes for granted. His own
bed and the freedom to luxuriate in peaceful sleep. A
hunted man never sleeps. A part of his mind always stays
alert to trouble.

He runs across the street and then keeps on running.
There are long stretches of open road on the way to the
Turneys. He has to keep low, move against the deepest
darkness he can find.

Dogs and coyotes; wagons and trains. The noises keep
up a running dialogue with the night.

But what if they turn him in?

But that's unthinkable. Not the Turneys. They'll know

he didn't do it. As religious as they are, they are generally not quick to judge people. They'll give their old friend time to explain himself, to be heard.

A horse.

Somewhere behind him.

Coming up fast.

He pitches himself in a leaf-littered gulley still muddy from last Monday's hard rain.

He rolls all the way down the leafy, shallow gully and then lies completely still. Sweat is freezing on him now. His breath comes in raw, painful gasps.

A posse man could have spotted him. Closed in. He listens for the horse to slow. Fortunately, the rhythm of the horse's hooves cutting into sandy earth remains the same. Wherever the rider is going, he's going in a hell of a hurry.

Heart pounding. Head aching. So unreal, all of it, him in this gulley, Suzie Proctor in her grave. God. So unreal.

He gives the rider plenty of time to vanish into the dark distance, and then he stands up, brushing leaves from legs, chest, hips, and legs.

He needs to hurry more than ever. The Turney home has begun to assume a magnificence well beyond its reality. There he will find nurture and acceptance and understanding; there he will find comfort and solace and help. If only he can travel these last few miles without being seen.

He runs on. For the first time in his young life, he finds himself feeling old. He's barely twenty-three, but he can feel the incredible stress all this exercise has put on him. Even two years ago—even with his smoking and drinking—this wouldn't have been anything for him. But now . . .

He runs on.

He is just starting to feel good about things—he *will* escape—he *will* ultimately be found innocent—

—when somebody opens up with a carbine.

He's running along a leg of the moon-dappled river when somebody from behind one of the birches lining this side of the shore starts firing.

One of the first three shots comes so close to his face that he can *smell* it.

Two more shots.

He dives and rolls. He doesn't know what else to do. Dive and roll, all the gunslingers always suggest in dime novels. That's about the only thing a man can do when somebody is ambushing him.

The only thing these supposedly knowledgeable gunfighters don't mention in their stories is how hard diving and rolling is on the body. Solid earth doesn't give any when a human body collides with it.

He's just had to roll down a ravine. And now he's diving and rolling? Being a fugitive is damned hard work.

After his body has been jolted, rattled, and shocked enough, he crawls to his knees, gets behind a boulder, and begins to take a little target practice of his own. His assailant doesn't seem to realize that the moonlight makes him a reasonably easy target.

Bobby is gratified to hear the man cry out in pain.

The sweetest sound he's heard in some time.

8:48 P.M.

Ben Gregg was walking toward his hotel when he saw Virgil Earp hurrying from the town marshal's office. His mount was ready for him. He was about to swing up on it when he saw Ben.

He walked over and said, "Your brother was holed up at Serena's place."

"How'd you find that out?"

"My deputy, Sam. Your brother knocked him out."

"I take it he's on the run?"

"That's the way Sam tells it."

Ben nodded to Earp's horse. "You have any idea where he might be hiding?"

"Nope. I just hope I find him before the posse does."

"They still working this late?"

Earp shook his head. "The other two posses came in and gave up. They're pretty much tired of lookin' for him. But there's six or seven of the boys who're still lookin'. And now they're in town here. I guess they decided I wasn't so stupid after all, him holin' up at Serena's place all this time." He made a face. "The other thing is, they stopped off at a trail saloon about five miles east of here and drank most of the afternoon. They probably tied a pretty good mean on too."

"You could always call them in."

"Not where Suzie Proctor's concerned, Gregg. Just about everybody liked her and they sure want to see her killer caught."

"Maybe I'll look for him myself."

"How about you?" Earp said. "*You* got any ideas?"

"Afraid not."

"Well, if you find him, bring him in."

"I will, Marshal." And he would too. He'd rather take a chance with Earp and Earp's jail than with a gang of drunks.

BEN WATCHED THE marshal ride off and then went up to his room. The moment he opened the door, he knew that somebody was inside waiting for him. The perfume told him so.

"You need to keep the lamp off. For both our sakes."

"Who're you?"

"My name's Serena. I am in love with your brother."

"Where is he?"

"I'm not sure. But I have an idea."

"Where?"

She sighed. "Do you know the Turneys?"

"I just came from there."

"They're the only people in this town who'll help them."

"Besides you."

A hesitation. "I know I am in trouble. They already hate me here because I'm a whore. But I love him. I know that someday we'll have a family together. Or shouldn't I say that because I'm a whore?"

"Whore is a mental state."

"I don't understand."

He took his pipe from his suit jacket, tamped down the tobacco with his thumb, and got it going with a stick match. "In your mind and soul. If you feel like a whore there, then you are a whore. But if all that you give men is the use of your body—and you don't cheat them or hurt them or hurt yourself—then I reckon there're are worse things to be."

She laughed. "I should have you along when the town girls call me names."

"I'd be happy to go." Then: "Shouldn't you be at work?"

"I quit tonight."

"How'll you support yourself?"

"We're through around here anyway, your brother and I. We'll go somewhere else and start a new life."

He found it strange that a woman with such sure ideas wouldn't have come up once in his brother's letters. The kid was forever falling in and out of love, but he'd never once talked about Serena.

He said, "I'm going to ask you something and I'd appreciate an honest answer."

"All right."

"You think he killed her?"

"That Bobby killed Suzie?"

"Yes."

"No. No, he wouldn't do anything like that. Ever."

"He drinks."

"Yes."

"And sometimes he has a bad temper."

She looked cold, hard angry. "He didn't kill her."

"Good enough."

"Certainly you can't think he killed her."

"People always surprise me. Sometimes for the bad and sometimes for the good. It makes you lie awake some nights and just think about things."

"He didn't kill her, Mr. Gregg. He didn't kill her."

He said, "You'd better go. I'd better check out the Turneys' place again. He has to give himself up before that posse finds him."

"I'll go with you."

"No."

She stood up. "You can't stop me. If I want to follow you, I can. You might as well take me along."

He said, "I don't mean to hurt your feelings here, but are you sure my brother's in love with you?"

"Not yet, he isn't. But he will be and very soon now. Some men are just very slow learners, and Bobby is one of them."

He liked her more than he might have expected. She was a little hard, but she had an honesty and dignity he admired. It wasn't easy to have any self-respect in her chosen calling, but somehow she did. Nobody pushed her around or took advantage of her. But given Bobby's history with women, he wasn't sure she was going to get her man.

"You do exactly what I say."

"Fine by me," she said.

He looked out the window. "We'll have to go out the back way."

"Why?"

"Virgil Earp's got one of his deputies stationed across the street. I'm sure he's ready to follow us."

"What if there's a deputy in back?"

"Then you'll have to do a little dramatic presentation and divert him."

"What're you talking about?"
"You'll see."

9:09 P.M.

Turney was just putting the cat out for the night when he
heard the scuffle of a boot on dry earth outside in the
night. Alarmed, he looked hard to the right and saw nothing. Then he looked to the left.

"You've got to help me, Richard," Bobby Gregg said.

Turney hardly recognized the man. Sweat, dirt, mud,
even leaves covered various parts of his body. Even from
a distance of four yards, Turney could smell the sour body
odors.

"They're looking for you, Bobby." He didn't know
what else to say. He felt guilty. As if Bobby could read
his mind, knew all about Jean Anne's notion to blame
Bobby for the murder and keep Richard free. He swal-
lowed hard. Bobby might have been a ghost, he'd rattled
Richard so hard.

Gregg surprised him by smiling. "Hell, Richard, you
think I don't know that?"

"Who's there, Richard?" Jean Anne said from inside.

Richard waved Bobby inside.

BOBBY KNEW INSTANTLY that something was wrong.
Soon as he stepped inside. The first thing was, they kept
backing away from him. They were usually physical people. They patted shoulders, gave hugs, Jean Anne was
even known to put a kiss on your cheek from time to
time. But now they were wary of him, as if he was a
disease-carrier. And they kept glancing anxiously at each
other, as if responding to a secret only they knew. And
then he realized what this was probably all about. Of
course. They probably believed he'd killed her. Sure, that
was why they were acting this way. You have a good
friend for a number of years—a solid, honest, decent

friend, one you think you know pretty well—and then he suddenly kills a woman. The woman he loves, no less. And so things change. He becomes a monster. And he's standing right in your own kitchen. Asking for help. No wonder they looked scared and nervous.

He said, "I didn't kill her. I want you to know that."

"Everybody sure thinks you did," Jean Anne said.

"Does that include you?"

Her eyes avoided his. "No."

He said, "It does, docsn't it? You believe I killed her and so does Richard here. That's why you're acting this way."

"We don't know what to think, Bobby," Jean Anne said. "We kept telling people over and over you were innocent. But when so many people believe something—"

"When so many people believe something, it must be true, is that it?"

"Something like that," she said miserably. "You talk to him, Richard."

Richard said, "Maybe it'd be better if I fetched Virg Earp."

"They'd still lynch me. They'd go over him if they had to. Or hell, he might just let them hang me, an election comin' up and all."

"Then what's the alternative, Bobby?"

"Running," he said. "For right now that's the only alternative anyway. Running. But I need a bath and some fresh clothes and some money."

The look again, passing between them.

"We could get in trouble."

Bobby smiled. "Yeah, Jean Anne, you could get in trouble. But I could get lynched." In some ways, it was hard to believe that they'd ever been friends. He remembered so many good times with these people. Hell, he was the little boy's godfather. But that was gone from him now. They'd never be friends again.

"We could at least do that for him," Richard said.

"Some fresh clothes. And some money. He could scrub up at the sink over there."

"I'd appreciate it," Bobby said.

"You might, but the law won't, Bobby. Earp'll get on us for helping you escape."

"We have to help him, honey, he's our friend."

"Some friend," Jean Anne said. "He kills a woman and then comes here and wants us to help him."

And it was then she figured out the way to handle this whole thing. She had a Navy Colt in her drawer. She'd kill Bobby with it. There'd be reward money and the case would be closed. No more questions asked.

She sighed. "Oh, all right. I'm sorry if I sounded unfriendly, Bobby. I'm just scared is all."

"I really appreciate this," Bobby said. "It's the only chance I've got."

Richard found him clothes. Jean Anne set up the sink so he could give himself a good sponge bath. She went to the drawer with the gun. It was also where they kept their cash box. There was eighty dollars in there. Everything they had. She'd give Bobby thirty. It'd be good when her money was found on him. It would demonstrate that they really *had* been trying to help him escape. But had been forced to shoot him when he demanded every penny of their savings. Virg Earp would have no reason to disbelieve them.

She stayed in the bedroom until she heard Bobby dumping out the water he'd used to bathe in.

Then she hid the gun in the folds of her farm skirt and went out to face him.

9:30 P.M.

"You did that well."

"My hip hurts."

"Well, I just wanted you to know that I appreciated it."

"I just hope we're not too late."

Serena was hobbling. She'd gone out the back door of the hotel first. She made a big thing of being drunk and falling on her face. The deputy—never one to pass up a cheap feel—went to her assistance immediately. Filling his hands with her swelling breasts, he managed to get her to her feet and steady her. For which she was appreciative enough to touch her lips to his in a pretense of lusty drunkenness.

The splendid performance allowed Ben Gregg to sneak out the back door and clear of the deputy. Serena, hobbling because of the hip injury she'd suffered when she'd thrown herself gallantly to the ground, caught up with Ben ten minutes later.

Now they were near the railroad tracks that ran north-south. Far in the distance you could hear a train thundering down the tracks like some mythic nocturnal beast. Indian art often depicted trains with the totem-like faces of monsters, all red glowing eyes and steam pouring from nostrils and mouths. Indian children were no doubt told that if they did not behave, the train monster would get them.

"Trains scare me," Serena said.

"Why?"

She shuddered. "My uncle once saw a woman get her head cut off when she fell underneath a train. He used to tell us over and over about it."

"Just the kind of fella you'd like to have around."

They climbed a small, sandy hill. Below them, in a small, tree-ringed valley, lay the small, tree-ringed house of the Turney family, window-dark in the starry night.

Somebody was coming out the front door.

Ben had one of those moments when the brain refuses to accept the information the eyes are relaying.

Yes, this was a young man who did bear some resemblance to his brother Bobby. Yes, that strange kind of lope was the distinctive walk of the entire Gregg family. And true, the flat-brimmed dark blue Stetson looked unique even half-lost in the shadows this way.

But how could it be so easy? As a Pinkerton man, Ben Gregg was used to things being done the hard way. You walk to the rise of a small hill and there, not a hundred yards away, is the brother you've been desperately searching for?

No. Impossible.

But it was Bobby. No doubt about it. And the way Serena clutched Ben's arm confirmed what eye was telling brain.

And then something even more unlikely happened: Jean Anne Turney, devout Christian woman that she was, flung herself through the cabin door and screamed, "Bobby!"

Her intentions were as clear as the six-shooter in her hand. Just as Bobby was turning toward her voice, she was firing.

Then Ben heard himself shout: "Bobby! Bobby!" and was running down the hill with his gun drawn, firing at Jean Anne Turney before she could squeeze off any more shots.

Then Richard Turney ran out the front door crying, "Jean Anne, what're you doing? What're you doing?"

By now, Ben Gregg had reached the cabin and was kneeling down next to his brother. He shouted to Turney, "Get me a lantern!"

Turney didn't have to take the six-shooter from his wife. In a deep state of shock, her eyes looking off into some distance only she could see, she let the weapon drop from her fingers. He picked it up.

While Turney was getting a lantern, Ben said to Serena, "Would you go get Virgil Earp? Turney won't mind if you take one of his horses."

She hurried away.

Turney returned moments later with a glowing kerosene lantern.

Jean Anne rushed up to him as he stood over Bobby's body. "Is he dead? Did I kill him? Oh, Lord, I'm so sorry."

Turney handed the lantern to Ben. "She was doing it to protect me. I killed Suzie Proctor. But since everybody thought Bobby did, she thought nobody'd question her killing him."

Ben only half-heard what Turney was saying. He was more interested—at least for the moment—in Bobby's wound. It was high, in the shoulder. The blood flow was warm and thin. You could smell it on the chill night.

"How is he, Mr. Gregg?" Jean Anne said. "Oh, Lord, I'm so sorry. He was our best friend."

Bobby's eyes came open then and he said, "Yeah, best friend, all right. Some best friend." Ben had seen this many times. Somebody is shot, slips into unconsciousness, then suddenly comes to again after a few minutes.

"Should we take him inside?" Jean Anne said.

"I don't want to ever step inside your house again," Bobby said. He was strong enough to express anger with real passion.

Ben took off his suit jacket and laid it across Bobby blanket-style. He put Bobby's hat underneath his head, propping it up slightly. At least it wouldn't be lying directly upon the cold hard earth.

Ben stood up. From the doorway of the Turney home, Ruth watched them. He wondered if she could hear what was being said. That her father was the killer.

"You'll need to take care of things, Jean Anne," he said.

She started to cry. Her face in her hands. Turney took her into his arms. "I'm so sorry for everything I've done," he said. "I've brought God's wrath down on myself—and now my whole family's suffering. I just pray that you can forgive me someday, honey. I just hope you can forgive me."

Ben kept putting off what he needed to do. Every time

he was about to speak, one of the Turneys would say something very emotional and Ben would lay back again. During the last exchange, they moved downhill further, so that Ben couldn't hear them.

"I'm freezing my ass off down here, brother," Bobby said in the windy prairie night.

"Your girlfriend should be back with Earp and the wagon right away." He got down on his haunches and pulled his suit jacket up tighter around his brother.

"She ain't my girlfriend."

"She tells a different story. And anyway, you could do a lot worse. I like her."

Bobby grimaced with the pain from his shoulder. "Yeah, that's the hell of it."

"What is?"

"I like her, too. She kind of snuck up on me. I kinda knew Suzie was sneaking around on me, so I started spendin' time with Serena. I sure never figured it'd go anywhere, her bein' a whore and all."

"Mr. Gregg?"

He looked up. Ruth stood there. She said, "I'd like to talk to you."

"You be all right?"

Bobby nodded. "Can't get any colder than I am right now."

"You could always go inside."

"No way."

"All right. I'll talk to the young lady, then."

He stood up, knees cracking. Every once in a while he got the sneaking suspicion that one of these days he was actually going to get old.

You could see the sleep on her face. She'd apparently slept at least a while tonight. She was as pretty as her mother, her gentle face pale in the moonlight.

She said, "I killed her, Mr. Gregg."

He sensed the great grief in her. Her father a killer. The only way she could help him was to take the blame herself. An absurd story. But a profoundly touching one.

He drew her into the circle of his arm. "Your father wouldn't want you to go around saying things like that, honey."

"But I did kill her, Mr. Gregg. I really did." Her tone was as chill as the night. "I knew they were over there by the river. They went there a lot. Sometimes, I sneak out of the house and go for walks at night. And one night I saw them together. And then I saw them a *lot* of nights. You know, they say she was such a fine person and all. But she wasn't. She was destroying my family and she didn't care at all. That's why he strangled her. Because she wouldn't let him go. I watched him strangle her. I was hiding behind the tree where I usually did. And then after he ran off, I went down there. I'm not even sure why. I'd never seen a dead person before. Maybe I was just interested in that. But anyway, I went down there and when I was leaning over, she opened her eyes and started to get up. And I just started screaming all these things at her. About how she was ruining my folks and everything. And then I just picked up this rock and I hit her with it. I hit her twice, as a matter of fact. And then I dropped it and ran back up to the house."

He'd wondered why she'd been both strangled and then hit with a heavy rock. Now he knew why. He also knew that Ruth was telling him the truth. He said, "You wore the shoes you usually do?"

"Yes, why?"

"Mind if I see your heel?"

"How come?"

"I need to see if there's a V imprinted there."

The V was there, all right. Imprinted in the heel itself.

"You think they'll hang me?"

The way she said it, so dispassionately, he wondered for the first time if she might be insane.

"No; no, they won't hang you, sweetheart."

"I just wanted my Dad to be home the way he should be."

"I know."

"My mom would never do anything like that to *him.*"

"No; no, she wouldn't."

Then she was in his arms and starting to cry. "I know I shouldn't have hit her; I know I shouldn't have, Mr. Gregg."

He let her cry for a time, and then he called out to the people down the hill, "You need to come up here, Mr. and Mrs. Turney."

Soon after, Virgil Earp and a hospital wagon for Bobby showed up too.

NEXT DAY, 2:37 P.M.

Serena sat in a chair next to Bobby's hospital bed. Ben stood on the other side saying, "It's a good thing you're my brother. Otherwise I would've charged Pinkerton rates."

"He thinks he has a great sense of humor," Bobby said.

"I should charge you too for all the peach pie you ate," Serena said. "You finished off the whole thing."

Bobby looked as if he was about to say something in his own defense, then stopped.

"What were you going to say?" she said.

"I can't say."

"You can't say what you were going to say? What kind of crazy talk is that?"

"I gave my word," Bobby said, thinking of Deputy Sam wolfing down the entire pie.

Older brother Ben patted his hand and said, "I need to go. Allegedly, my train leaves in another half hour."

"Allegedly?" Bobby said.

"You ever know a train to leave on time?" Ben said.

On his way to the depot, he ran into Deputy Sam carrying a pie to the hospital.

"This," Sam said, "is for your brother. I had my wife work all morning. It's peach."

"That's funny," Ben said. "Serena was just saying that Bobby ate this whole peach pie that *she* fixed."

"It's a small world, isn't it?" Sam said, and then took of scuttling toward the hospital.

A strange little burg, the Pinkerton man thought as he began walking toward the depot again. A strange little burg indeed.

The Story

~∞~

by Robert J. Randisi

Robert J. Randisi co-founded *Mystery Scene* magazine, single-handedly created the Private Eye Writers of America, and has created a number of cutting-edge anthologies showcasing contemporary hard-boiled fiction at its best. While Randisi's early crime novels were swift, sure, singular looks at working-class Brooklyn (two of which were deservedly nominated for Shamus awards), his more recent books demonstrate the true width and depth of his skills, in particular his novels about Detective Joe Keough, which include *East of the Arch*. He is also an excellent Western writer, with a number of novels to his credit in that genre, most notably perhaps *The Ham Reporter*, about Bat Masterton's days in New York City as a sports reporter.

1

OCTOBER 21, 1881

JOHN CALDER'S HEART started to beat a little faster as the stage pulled into Tombstone. Outwardly, however, he appeared calm. Calder considered this to be a strength of his. No one could ever tell how he was feeling from his outward appearance. His father had once told him,

"Your emotions are your own business, John. No one need ever know what's going on inside of you." He had always taken this advice to heart, as he did most of the things his father told him. His father might have been a bully, and a selfish man, but he was also very, very smart.

He thought of his father now, sitting in his private club with his wealthy colleagues, a cognac in one hand, the other being used to turn the pages of one of the many Western newspapers he subscribed to—as many he could get his hands on. A rich and successful banker in Boston, Winston Calder was very impressed by the "shootists" who lived—and died—in the Wild West. This was something else John Calder knew only too well, for he had been secretly taking those newspapers when his father was finished with them and reading them himself. This was the only way he had finally been able to figure out how to impress his old man.

When the stage came to a halt, John Calder allowed the other three passengers to step from it first. He knew who they all were not because he had conversed with them, but because he had listened to them speak with each other. There were two men, one a drummer and the other a lawyer. There was also a woman who claimed to be an "entertainer." She was pretty enough to be an actress, a saloon girl, or a whore, but Calder cared little which one it actually was.

Actually, who any of these people were and what they were doing in Tombstone meant very little to Calder. He had eavesdropped on them only to relieve his own boredom, and to distract himself from the smell. No one had told him that the West would be so dusty, and smell so bad. Why didn't the newspapers write about that?

While the other passengers gathered their baggage, Calder stepped out of the coach himself. He turned in time to catch his carpetbag, which the driver had rudely dropped down to him. Only his quick hands had kept the bag from braining him. He hadn't packed very much.

What he had to do in Tombstone should not take him very long. Of course, what he *had* packed had been chosen very carefully indeed. Next, the driver dropped a hatbox, which had been an unavoidable part of Calder's travel accessories. It had attracted strange looks more than once on the train, as well as the stage, but he had ignored them.

The stage had stopped right in front of the Grand Hotel, which made choosing a hotel easy. He entered and approached the front desk. The woman who had been on the stagecoach with him was also registering, so he had to wait his turn. When she was finished, she turned abruptly and bumped into him. Under other circumstances, it would have been an enjoyable bump, but he was extremely focused on the purpose of his journey.

"Oh, I'm sorry," she said, then seemed to recognize him. Closer still than they had been within the confines of the coach, he saw that she had violet eyes with small lines in the corners. Not as young as she would like people to think, she was also wearing very heavy makeup in an attempt to hide those lines. Trying to impress, he thought.

"Well, hello," she said.

"Hello," he replied, although they had not exchanged any words previously.

"Will you be staying here?"

"Hopefully," he said, "if they have rooms available."

"Well," she said, speaking with just a hint of a Southern accent he was certain was fake, "I certainly hope I didn't get the last one. Perhaps we'll be neighbors."

"Perhaps," he said.

"Good luck."

She walked away and he stepped up to the desk without watching her, as other men in the lobby were doing.

"And how can I help you, sir?" the clerk asked pleasantly.

"A room."

"Certainly, sir."

He was given a room on the second floor and carried his own bag up the stairs. He did not know or care what floor the woman had been put on.

2

NOW THAT HE was in Tombstone, all he had to do was determine if his target was still there. That meant he had to find the man who had sent him the telegram.

When Calder got to his room, he stopped just inside the door and looked around with distaste. The larger-than-life West had so far turned out to be such a disappointment, and this room did nothing to change that impression.

He put his bag on the sagging bed, and took out the clothing he had so carefully chosen from his father's favorite store in Boston. He unfolded each article and laid them out on the bed to inspect them. He smoothed them out until he was reasonably satisfied, then draped the pants and jacket over a straightbacked wooden chair in the corner. The starched white shirt he left folded and put into a dresser drawer along with his socks. Next, he took out the black boots, made of the best Italian leather, which he had polished to a high shine before packing them, and set them underneath the chair. That done, he tossed the valise into a corner along with the hatbox and left the room.

OUT ON ALLEN Street, Calder could see that everything he had heard about Tombstone was true. This was a wild town, and just right for what he needed to do. He strolled Allen Street, eyeing the saloons and gambling houses. He bypassed the Alhambra and opted for the Oriental, thinking he would find his man in the most opulent of places. Sure enough, he saw Frank O'Rourke lounging against the long mahogany bar, listening to the music of a violin and piano. O'Rourke was little more than a tinhorn gambler; he had delusions of grandeur about himself that fit the Oriental. He apparently had no illusions concerning his own appearance, however, for he had described himself to a T in his last telegram to John Calder. He was a small man with lank, dirty hair and clothing of the quality worn by homeless tramps on the streets of Boston. Those had not been his words, but the picture his words had brought to John Calder's mind—and now he saw how accurate his mind's eye had been.

John Calder approached the smaller man and tapped him on the shoulder. O'Rourke turned so quickly he spilled some of the beer from his mug.

"Who the hell—" the man stammered, a look of fright on his face.

"John Calder," he said, "from Boston."

"Hell, Calder! You, uh, surprised me. When'd you get in?"

"Just a little while ago," Calder said.

O'Rourke looked Calder up and down and said, "Yer a lot younger than I thought you'd be."

John Calder was twenty-four, but that was none of this rat-faced man's business.

"What have you got for me?"

O'Rourke moved closer, and Calder pulled his head back a few inches as a result of the smell. He didn't know what was worse, the man's body odor or his breath.

"You got no worries," O'Rourke said. "You're all set for your big day."

"Where?"

"There's a church at one end of town. You can't miss it. That's where he is."

"When?"

"Every day."

"In church?"

O'Rourke nodded and said, "In church."

"What is he—"

"He's a preacher now. Preaches the word of the Lord every day at noon."

"A preacher?" John Calder was taken aback.

"Hey," O'Rourke said, "your poster said you was looking for a man with a shootist's reputation. That's what he's got. Shootist, is that a word you fellas in the East use?"

"What kind of reputation—"

"See," O'Rourke said, "he put down his guns and came here to preach to the sinners of Tombstone. I guess he thought he needed to spread the Good Word in one of the worst hellholes in the West. Well, he got his wish." O'Rourke took a healthy swallow of beer, pouring some of it down his chin and chest in the process. "You got my money?" His piggy little eyes were feverish with greed, and beer dripped from the point of his chin. John Calder had an overwhelming desire to get away from the man. He took some bills from his pocket and handed them to Frank O'Rourke, then turned to leave.

"You don't wanna stay for a beer?" the man asked.

Calder turned back slowly and looked at him, then turned away and left without another word.

3

THE FOLLOWING MORNING, Calder rose early and arranged for a hot bath before breakfast. He had a leisurely soak in the tub, and then a large breakfast of steak and eggs, biscuits and gravy. He ate as leisurely as he bathed, and he was feeling better than he had any time since he'd come West.

Then it was time to go to church.

THE SUIT HE wore to church was serviceable, nothing like the one that was waiting in his room. He took a seat in the back, and sat quietly while the man in the pulpit

preached about fire and brimstone. Calder wondered if
any of the people there knew that the man used to dis-
pense it from the barrel of his gun.

During the service, his mind wandered back to Boston.
He wondered what his father thought when he first missed
him, when he didn't show up at the bank to work his
window. That was the only job his father would give him
in his bank, a teller. He wanted his son to work his way
up the ladder, the way he had done. Only, John Calder
did not intend to be a mere teller for very long. Once he
had figured out exactly what it would take to impress his
father, he put his plan into effect. He sent the word out
and knew that some little person—a man like O'Rourke,
to whom a small reward was a fortune—would eventually
contact him and give him the news he was waiting for.
When it came, he wasted no time hopping a train, with
not a word to his father. There was no other family to be
concerned with, no brothers, no sisters, and his mother
had been dead seven years. No, the old man would not
hear it from anyone else, would not be aware of the news
until he read it in one of his precious western newspapers.

After the service was over and the people began to file
out, Calder remained in his seat. The preacher went to the
door to exchange pleasantries with his flock as they left,
and when he came inside, he saw Calder sitting there.

"Can I help you with something?" he asked, frowning.
"I don't recognize you. You're not one of my flock, are
you?"

"No, Preacher, I'm not," Calder said, "but you deliver
a mighty fine sermon. I might even have been newly con-
verted today if I didn't have something else on my mind."

"And is this something that is weighing heavily on
you?" the man asked. "Is it something I can help you
with?"

The preacher was tall and sturdily built, his hair short,
dark, shot with gray. Calder guessed him to be about
fifty—twice his own age, in fact. Calder could easily see

past the concerned look and the simple clothes to the man he had been before.

"Weighing heavily?" he repeated thoughtfully. "No, sir, I don't think so. It's just something that I have to do, but it does concern you, Preacher—and your gun."

"My . . . gun?" A steely look came into the preacher's eyes.

"The gun you've put away," Calder said, "but the one I'm sure you still have." Calder had read in dime novels how attached a man got to his gun, especially when he'd lived by it for so long.

"What do you want?" the preacher asked.

"You," Calder said, "out on the street, after tomorrow's service."

A weary look came over the man's face.

"I suppose I knew this day would come," he said. "Is there anything I can say or do to change your mind about this?"

"I don't think so," Calder said. "You have no idea how much time and work I've put into this." Practicing with his Peacemaker, over and over and over, until he could draw it fairly quickly and fire accurately. After all, he should at least give the *appearance* of actually putting up a fight. What fun would it be to have his father simply read that he was shot down on a street in Tombstone like a dog? No, he had to read that he'd actually been killed *in a gunfight*. Then he would become one of those men his father admired, who lived by the gun—and died by it.

"What's your name?" the man asked him.

"John Calder."

"John Calder, you realize there's a very good chance I'll kill you, don't you?" the gunman-turned-preacher said.

"Oh yes, Preacher," Calder said, "I know that very well."

The preacher looked into his eyes and said, "I can see you're determined to die."

"Just be on the street, Preacher," John Calder said, "tomorrow, after services."

The preacher sighed and said, "All right. I'll be there."

"With your gun on."

"With my gun on."

"Excellent," John Calder said. "You have no idea what this means to me, Preacher."

"No," the man said, "I'm sure I don't."

AFTER JOHN CALDER left, the preacher sat in one of the pews and stared up at the podium where he'd stood just moments before, preaching to his flock. What would they think of him when he killed that young man tomorrow, right in front of the church? What would they think of everything he had been telling them for months? That they were all lies?

He shook his head. He could not have them think he was lying to them. If that were to happen, his time here would have been wasted. There was only one way to make sure that they remembered him as a preacher, and not as a liar and a gunman.

Only one way . . .

4

HIS SUIT WAS black, and had never been worn before. He had purchased it from the same place his father bought all his suits, especially for this opportunity. It was the most expensive suit of clothes he had ever owned. He donned the pants, found the length to be perfect. Next, he took the white shirt out of the dresser drawer. It was boiled white and crisp to the touch when he put it on, and the sleeves were exactly the right length. He fastened them with a pair of solid-gold cuff links. He took his time tying his tie, getting it perfect, admiring the way he looked in the mirror, and then added a diamond stickpin. He then took the suit jacket from the back of the wooden chair and slipped into it, then shot his cuffs to make sure the gold was visible. He looked in the mirror again. It had been tailored especially for him and fit perfectly. It did not in any way inhibit the movement of his arms, which was important. He looked better than any bridegroom he had ever seen.

Now the hat. He picked up the hatbox, opened it, and took out the flat-brimmed black hat with the silver-dollar band he'd bought from his father's favorite gentlemen's shop. He placed it on his head, tilted both the hat and his head until it looked right, then stepped back to try and see as much at one time as he could.

Perfect.

All that was left was the gun and gun belt at the bottom of the valise. He took it out, unfurled it, and strapped it on beneath the jacket. He had gone to Boston's finest gun shop, but instead of buying the newest weapon available, he'd had the man find him the weapon that had tamed the West—the Peacemaker. The gun and belt were somewhat worn, and he imagined that at one time or another they had adorned the person of some famous gunman—and now they were on his hip.

Lastly came his new black boots. The shine on the fine Italian leather was high enough for him to see his reflection, and the heels were just the right height, adding perhaps two inches to his own.

When he stood up, he attended to the finishing touch to his outfit—he strapped on his holstered Colt .45. Maybe he was going to church, but the gun was what was going to make all of this work.

Satisfied that he looked as good as he possibly could, he put on the flat-brimmed black hat he had bought just for this occasion and walked down to the lobby. He was so dressed up that he got looks from people in the lobby. When he stepped outside, he got many of the same looks from people he passed on the street. They probably thought he was either a preacher, a gambler, or a bridegroom.

IT WAS TWELVE-THIRTY when he reached the church. Standing at the top of the steps was the preacher, standing just in front of the church doors. His flock had been and gone; he stood there alone.

The preacher who wasn't always a preacher smiled.

"You think killing me is going to make you a big man, John Calder? Make a name for you?"

"You have no idea what I think, Preacher," Calder said. His hands were sweating, his heart was racing, but he actually felt more alive than he had in his life. What would happen, he thought, if I won? If he killed the preacher instead of the other way around? What were the chances of that? Next to none? Still, it was an exciting prospect.

"What will you do then?" the preacher asked. "Once you're famous?"

Calder shrugged and said, "Enjoy it."

The preacher shook his head.

"These people only know me as their preacher, John Calder," the man said. "There will be no fame in this for you. Just a lot of explaining for you to do."

"Come down the steps, Preacher," Calder said. "Stand on even ground with me."

The preacher obeyed, descending the steps. Calder saw with satisfaction that the man was wearing both his guns, a pearl-handled revolver on each hip. His trademark.

"Well," the preacher said when he reached the bottom of the steps, "at least you look like you're dressed for a funeral."

Funeral? That was one thing Calder hadn't thought of, but it certainly made sense.

"Your funeral maybe," Calder said. Might as well make a show of thinking he could actually win this thing.

People were beginning to gather, to watch with curiosity to see what was developing.

"You think you're going to get your picture taken for this, don't you?" the preacher asked.

"Enough talk," Calder said. "Let's just do it."

"I'll give you one last chance to walk away, John Calder."

"I can't do it, Preacher," Calder said. "There's too much at stake."

"I didn't think you would," the other man said, "but for my own conscience, I had to give you the chance."

They fell silent then, and faced each other in the sun, people on either side of the street stopping to watch.

Calder had no idea who should make the first move. He watched the preacher and waited as long as he could, but impatience got the better of him. He drew his gun and fired. It was a shock to him that he even got to pull the trigger. He'd expected to be gunned down before he could clear leather. Instead, he pulled the trigger and his shot went true and struck the preacher in the chest. The man staggered and dropped both of his pearl-handled revolvers into the dirt of Allen Street. He wavered there for a moment; then Calder thought he saw him smile before he fell facedown on top of his guns.

"It was a fair fight," John Calder said from behind bars.

"That's what you say," the man with the pencil and pad replied.

"You make sure your readers know who he really was," Calder said. "I gave you his name."

"Yes, you did," said Arthur Pryor, the editor of the *Tombstone Nugget*. "And quite a famous name it is too. Only . . ."

"Only what?"

"Only, that man is supposed to be dead, long dead," the editor said.

"You get ahold of Frank O'Rourke," Calder said.

"He's the one who told me about him. He knows who he really is."

"That's what you told the sheriff," Pryor said, "and he's looking for O'Rourke right now, but you're gonna have to go to trial, son."

"That's okay," Calder said, "just you make sure you write this all up. The only thing that's important is that you write the story."

"Oh, I'll write it up, all right," the editor said, "don't you worry about that."

"When will your paper be out?" Calder asked anxiously.

"Well, we ain't a daily," Pryor said, "but don't you worry, it'll be out soon enough."

"Front page?"

"It would take somethin' mighty big to knock the killing of our preacher off the front page, son," Pryor said.

"Thank you, Mr. Pryor," Calder said, extending his hand through the cell for the editor to shake. "I appreciate it."

The editor withdrew his hand and said, "I don't understand it."

"You don't have to," Calder said. "You just have to write the story."

AFTER THE EDITOR left, John Calder sat on his cot. This was not the way he had expected it to happen. He'd thought he would be killed, and his father would read about it in the newspaper and be impressed. Moments after the shooting, he had patted down his own body, looking for wounds, and was shocked to find none. So shocked that he had not moved by the time the sheriff arrived, disarmed him, and took him into custody. He was more shocked at being alive than he was at the fact that he'd killed the other man. It had been remarkably easy, he thought now, as if the other man had not even tried.

It was he, after all, who was the storied gunman. And what was that smile about just before he died?

John Calder still did not understand everything that had happened, but the fact remained that this entire affair—the shooting, the arrest, the trial, and his acquittal—would all come out in the newspaper—in one of his father's precious Western newspapers.

And that, after all, was the whole point.

IT WAS NOT until October 27th that the *Tombstone Nugget* finally hit the street, and by that time the front page was taken up with the headline GUNFIGHT AT O.K. COR-RAL, and the corresponding story of the savage battle that had taken place between the Earps and the Clantons.

Buried on page six, in a small column, was a hastily written story, very short on facts, about an unknown gunman who had been hanged for killing the town preacher, after he had forced the poor man into a gunfight. It was a sketchy story at best, but then who was going to read anything other than that front-page story?

Hangman's Choice

∽∾∽

by Loren D. Estleman

Loren D. Estleman is generally considered the best Western
writer of his generation. Such novels as *Aces & Eights, The
Stranglers,* and *Bloody Season* rank with the very best Western novels ever written. As will be seen here, Estleman
brings high style to his writing, the sentences things of
beauty in and of themselves. Few writers of prose can claim
that. He has brought poetry, historical truth, and great wis-
dom to the genre. His finest short Western fiction was collected in *The Best Western Stories of Loren D. Estleman.*

OSCAR STONE LOOKED at the glossy red Concord coach
standing before the Wells Fargo office in Tucson, and
realized for the first time that he was growing old.

He was, in fact, only thirty-four, a young age back
East, where men of his intelligence and ability moved
railroads and sank mine shafts all across the continent
from behind big mahogany desks until they were too weak
and brittle to lift a pen; but the frontier was a youngster's
venue—scourged, tamed, and maintained by men whose
life expectancy was thirty, if they hadn't made their for-
tunes by then and shipped back to Chicago and New
York. There was a time, just after the war, when the bare
miracle of his survival had convinced him he was equal

to any hardship, and if it involved fighting Indians or out-witting bandits or swinging a heavy pick all day against unresisting rock, he would endure and outlive all his wounds and bruises and sore, screaming muscles with cash in the bank. Now the very thought of bouncing over many miles of undeveloped country with nothing between him and the rocks but four wheels and a leather strap made him bone-weary before the journey had even begun.

It was his own fault, he reminded himself; both for accepting an assignment in a place as wild and distant as Tombstone, and for allowing himself to become depend-ent upon the steadily improving railway system in the places where he'd been working his trade for years. Dur-ing the trip from Denver, he'd enjoyed the space and com-fort of seats in a series of Pullman cars, smoking cigars with his feet propped up on padded rests and making reg-ular visits to the dining car, never suspecting that the com-forts to which he'd grown accustomed had not yet extended to the richest silver-mining city in the world. When the station master in Tucson had informed him that from that point on he would be riding in a stagecoach— a discomfort to which he had not subjected himself in ten years—it had required the last shred of his professional ethic to avoid sending a wire to the sheriff of Comanche County canceling his visit and buying a ticket on the next train back to Denver.

He smiled thinly when the baggage handler stationed on the boardwalk accepted his Gladstone in both hands and passed it up gently to the man atop the coach, as if it contained fragile instruments or something of substan-tial value. In his well-cut gray suit with its quiet stripe, rolled hat brim, and gold-rimmed spectacles, Stone was often mistaken for a doctor or a banker. Had the man known what the bag contained and suspected its purpose, he'd have flung it up as quickly as possible, and perhaps wiped his hands before bending to the next. Pioneers feared almost nothing in the nature of physical danger, but reverted to superstitious childhood when a black cat or a hearse crossed their paths.

The handler assured him he had time to lunch, and recommended the dining room of the Commonwealth Hotel. At a pleasant table covered with a checked cloth, he spent some minutes studying the bill of fare, and twice as long discussing his selections with the waiter, whom he had difficulty convincing that his meal must contain no meat. The result was a bland arrangement of cauliflower overcooked into a lukewarm slush, tinned tomatoes, and watery onion soup, washed down with wine that tasted depressingly like gun oil; the sediment clung like tea leaves to the bottom of the glass. He was accustomed to such disappointment, however. Frontier chefs, some of whom compared with the best of Europe, seldom concerned themselves with the fine points of preparing vegetables, and he could hardly expect to encounter a Boston claret or a Madeira the way they were served in San Francisco. It was Apache country, after all.

He consoled himself with a creditable cup of coffee and considered his fellow diners. Here was a cowboy with his hair slicked down and a clean shirt buttoned to the throat, attacking a pork chop with obvious enjoyment; his sunburned features indicated he'd been eating stringy beef and prairie onions for many weeks on a cattle drive from old Mexico. There, with napkins tucked under their detachable collars to protect their starched shirtfronts, were a pair of wealthy ranchers, discussing the rustling problem in loud voices over slabs of ham swimming in a wine sauce—made, Stone hoped, from some vintage older than the one that was souring his own stomach at present. In the corner sat a young man in a stiff new suit and a pretty girl in calico, more interested in one another than they were in the contents of their plates; a courtship ritual in full flower.

Man and boy, the traveler had spent his life among the fresh-built metropolises, homely pueblos, and sod way stations of the West, observing without participating, understanding without joining, no more a part of what he saw than a Chicago clubman nodding in his armchair over a stereoscope and slides. It was the nature of the work he had chosen, and whatever pain it caused was fleeting, like the taste of cauliflower left to simmer too long. In a somber study, he paid his bill and presented himself again before the express office.

His fellow passengers diverted him for the first twenty minutes of his journey, after which he found more interest in the scenery outside the window: essentially the same arrangement of brick-colored rocks and parched vegetation he'd been looking at ever since he crossed into Arizona Territory. He missed the determined men and brave women with whom he'd traveled in years past, who had turned their backs on the things they knew and people they'd loved in search of a new life in the uncharted vastness of what was then known as the Great American Desert. Tales of hostile Indians, highwaymen, grizzlies, and extremes of climate had winnowed out the unworthy and faint-hearted, leaving the best that a country seeking to heal itself after four years of war had to offer. Fifteen years of railroad-building and spreading civilization had begun to draw the lesser lights from their overstuffed parlors: braying drummers in loud checked suits, mousy mail-order brides with cunning eyes, and fat, dyspeptic bankers and their disagreeable wives. Stone had not thought them worth the breath required to tell them the purpose of his visit, merely explaining that he was bound on "county business."

Mercifully, this led to a discussion of Comanche County politics between the male passengers, from which he was able to extricate himself with a confession that he had missed the wire accounts in the newspapers. He gathered from what followed that a heated contest for sheriff had turned dangerous when armed men on both sides had begun to threaten one another.

The conversation was not compelling enough to distract him from the discomforts of stagecoach travel. He had heard some of the same stories, with varying details, in Dodge City and Abilene and Cheyenne and other towns whose names he could no longer remember. Even some of the players were the same, belonging to that breed of two-legged wolf that migrated from one sudden town to another, muzzles to the wind for the scent of gold and blood. Tombstone, two days' ride from the nearest organized territorial law and a short hop from the border of old Mexico, was merely the latest sinkhole into which the scum of the prairie had settled, roiling with its petty jealousies and spilling its burning bile onto innocent onlookers and into the smutty black headlines of the national press.

If Stone had wanted to bother himself to follow the columns, he would have been able to predict six months ahead of time where his calling would take him. He had, in fact, once been an eager reader of newspapers, but of late entertained himself with the works of Charles Dickens and Oscar Wilde, whose characters were less predictable and offered more variety than the brigands and killers and politicians whose adventures never seemed to pall with reporters. In those earlier days, he had managed to convince himself that in his own small way he helped to stem the wicked tide. Now he just went where he was asked and did what he was paid to do, and contented himself with the knowledge that none did it better.

This was not the comfort it had been. It was the opposite, in fact. For months he'd toyed with the idea of retirement. Money was no longer a concern; he was paid as well as most senators, and the departure of his wife many years before had left him with no one but himself to spend it on, and his needs were simple. His account in the Cattleman's Bank of Chicago, upon which he drew an occasional draft for expenses, would keep him modestly for the rest of his life. He did not fear idleness. In his youth he'd been a master carpenter and cabinetmaker; the vista of all the tables, bureaus, book presses, and scroll-top desks he would fit and sand and hand-rub stretched pleasantly before him. But when he thought of what might happen to his profession once he left it, of the witlings and charlatans who flew his colors and would move in like the vermin they were to fill the space he left, he felt a chill that made his bones shudder in the desert heat. He would not abandon the field to their kind of evil.

The way station where they stopped for fresh horses and rest was an adobe hovel with a corral behind, built of the warped poles common in a land where lumber was dear. They were served tortillas and stew—Stone declined the stew—by the station operator's large Mexican wife at a pine table bleached white from many scrubbings, and shared news of the cities they had passed through in return for the latest on Geronimo and the situation in Tombstone. The shotgun messenger, a small, bald-headed Irishman with young eyes in a weathered face, asked about bandits.

"Thick as fleas." The station operator was a white man less than half his wife's size, but all knotted sinew where his forearms stuck out of his rolled shirtsleeves. "They hit the Benson run last month, killed the driver and a passenger. You want to watch yourself on that stretch."

"Well, we're not carrying bullion this trip."

"That don't mean nothing to this bunch. If it rolls or walks or crawls on its belly, they'll stomp it and pick its bones."

"And get a double load of buckshot in the face for their trouble." The Irishman patted his Stevens ten-gauge.

The driver came in to announce the horses were ready, and used a tortilla to scoop stew from his bowl without sitting down while the passengers filed out to reboard.

"The man in Tucson said we'd have a half hour to eat and rest," complained the banker's wife.

"I'll warrant he told you it was a smooth ride too. Put your hat on, Riley, and let's go. The damn Apaches can see the glare off your head for forty miles."

Dark had fallen when they reached the town of Benson. They overnighted at a boardinghouse run by a tiny woman with a sour face that seemed to have curdled the chicken and dumplings she served for supper and petrified the yolks of the eggs she fried at breakfast. (Stone satisfied himself both times with biscuits and coffee.) Then they were off for the last leg of the trip.

Stone had slept fitfully on a feather bed whose stuffing had migrated to the four corners of the ticking. Despite the pitching of the coach, he was falling asleep when a noise like the bark of a close dog jerked him awake. As his head cleared, he realized it was a gunshot he'd heard. The coach was rocking to a halt. There was no sign of civilization outside, just more red rock and clumps of yucca. The banker, a muttonchopped old dragon in a new duster and garish yellow gaiters, had produced a small silver pistol from a vest pocket. Outside, raised voices told Stone what it was about before he could understand what was being said.

"Indians?" The drummer clutched the sample case in his lap as if it contained his scalp.

"Worse," said the banker. "Bandits."

His wife clutched at his arm. "Oh, August, please put the gun away. They'll shoot you."

Stone said, "She makes good sense. We don't know how many there are."

Small eyes glared in the dragon face. "What do you know about it?"

"I've had some experience with criminals."

The argument ceased when a face wearing a blue bandanna appeared suddenly in the window on Stone's side. Startled, the banker jerked the trigger. The report filled the coach and a jagged piece jumped out of the wooden frame next to Stone's head and landed in his lap. Someone cursed and the heavy barrel of an Army Colt came through the opening. The crackle of the hammer sounded dull in the echo of the blast from the banker's weapon. His wife's shriek was not so dull.

"Throw that little shit-piece out the window," came a voice from behind the bandanna. "I ain't kilt a man since breakfast."

The shiny revolver went through the window on the banker's side as if it had leapt out of his hand.

The Colt swept around slowly to take in all the passengers. It stopped when it came to Stone. The eyes above the bandanna were pale blue in a face burned brown as a tobacco plug. "Looks like we got two bankers aboard. You got a deposit to make too?"

Stone said, "I'm not armed. I'm not a banker either."

"Sawbones then. You almost had a patient. Get out, the four of you. Watch your step. I got a bad case of nerves." He swung open the door.

They stepped down, raising their hands without waiting to be told. The driver and the shotgun messenger were standing next to the horses, staring at another man in a bandanna who had them covered with a Winchester carbine. The driver had both hands up, the Irishman only one. His other arm hung bleeding at his side. The Stevens ten-gauge was nowhere in sight. Stone guessed it had fallen from his hands when he was shot.

Another masked man held the horse team, while yet another clambered atop the coach and began throwing down luggage from the rack. That made five, counting the man who would be holding the bandits' horses somewhere out of sight. It was a professional crew.

"Where's the strongbox?" demanded the blue-eyed man.

The driver grinned, showing spaces in his teeth. "You boys are shy on luck. There ain't none."

The man on top climbed down to the driver's seat and swung open the footboard. "Empty."

Blue Eyes sighed. "Get down here and turn these pilgrims inside out. They look good for a day's pay."

The banker had a money belt full of cash. They got jewelry off his wife and found a gold thimble in her reticule. The drummer had only a dollar in his wallet, but Blue Eyes' partner was thorough and plucked a fifty-dollar gold piece out of the man's right sock. He slammed the muzzle of a short-barreled Colt alongside the drummer's temple and kicked him in the ribs twice when he fell. Stone knew the snap of bone when he heard it. He himself gave up the roll of banknotes he carried for travel expenses without waiting to be threatened, and handed over his watch, a heavy gold one with a brass chain.

"It's got words scratched on it." The man showed it to Blue Eyes, who took it and told him to go through the bags.

The first one the man opened happened to be Stone's. He pulled out coil after coil of well-oiled hemp. "Must be a rope drummer," he muttered.

Blue Eyes peered at the engraving on the back of the watch. " 'To Oscar Stone, for services rendered the Court of Arkansas, August 12, 1880. I.P.' Who the hell's I.P.?"

"Isaac Parker," Stone said. "He's the federal judge at Fort Smith. I filled in for his regular man last year."

"Regular *what* man?"

"Hangman. The fellow was sick and the jail was over-crowded. Evidently my work satisfied the judge."

The man kneeling over the Gladstone bag let drop the ropes and sprang to his feet. He shook his hands violently, as if he'd had them in a heap of maggots.

Stone, staring into the blue eyes, recognized that familiar old mix of hatred and horror. He'd seen it in the eyes of dozens just before he pulled the black hood over their heads. He braced himself—and in the next moment lay crumpled next to the drummer with his left cheek stinging. It felt as if the Colt's barrel had laid it open to the bone. He huddled for the kick, but it didn't come. Instead he was dragged to his feet by the back of his collar and a fist struck him hard in the abdomen, wrapped around the handle of the revolver. His lungs emptied.

When his vision cleared, he saw the rest of his life reflected in the eyes above the bandanna. He felt the finger tense on the trigger, the cylinder turning.

The hammer snapped on a punk shell.

Blue Eyes backed away rapidly. He recocked the pistol, fired it into the air—this time it was a live round—and swiveled on his heel to include all the passengers in its range before anyone could move. Stone remained motionless, clutching at the door of the coach for support.

"Forget that!" Blue Eyes barked at the man who had gone through Stone's bag; he'd begun to unstrap a leather valise. "We're clearing out."

"I just started!"

"You just finished. Get moving." He backed around in a half circle, then when he was on the other side of the man with the Winchester, he turned and trotted toward the brush beside the road.

The man holding the coach horses said, "Give me a second to cut loose the team."

"No time!"

Winchester and the man who'd been going through the bags exchanged glances. Then the former directed the driver and shotgun messenger to get down on their bellies. They complied, and with a final warning sweep of the carbine's barrel along the line of passengers, Winchester backed toward the brush while his companions hurried ahead of him. A moment later, hooves pounded the earth going away.

Stone bent to help the bruised and bleeding drummer to his feet. His own cheek was wet and sticky and his left eye had swollen almost shut. His knees wobbled; it was difficult to determine who was giving whom the most support. The drummer, however, was deathly pale.

"That was one spooked desperado." The driver dusted himself off and turned to examine the shotgun messenger's wound.

"Just a nick," said the other, shaking loose. "Numbed me up for a minute. Them bad hats don't like misfires nor hangmen. That's double bad luck. You're lucky to be alive, mister." His tone told Stone his own feelings weren't all that different.

"I'm all right. This fellow needs a doctor."

"Someone should go after those outlaws." They were the banker's first words since leaving the coach.

"Someone will, soon as we get to Tombstone. Riley, seeing as how you're bullet-proof, you can stow those bags and let's get going." The driver swung himself up onto the seat.

ENTERING TOMBSTONE ON the gallop, the driver began shouting the details of the robbery to those who came out to greet the stagecoach, and by the time he drew rein in front of Dr. Matthews's office, the story had spread throughout the town. Only on the frontier, Stone reflected, did fire and bad news defy the laws of physics and logic so dramatically. As he and Riley helped the drummer up the steps, he spotted the driver in a boardwalk conference with a small man in a big sombrero with a star on his chest, whom he took to be the county sheriff. That individual was gone by the time they reached the landing, and as Stone rested in an armchair outside the consulting room, shouts and hoofbeats from outdoors confirmed that a posse was under way.

Matthews, graying prematurely but without distinction, came out after forty minutes carrying his bag, and washed and applied sticking-plaster to the hangman's torn cheek. He'd sent Riley home with his arm in a sling. The drummer, he reported, had sustained internal injuries and his survival was open to question. Stone wondered if the doctor's apparent lack of concern had anything to do with a framed document on one wall identifying him as the Cochise County coroner.

A room had been arranged at the Cosmopolitan Hotel

on Allen Street. Small but elegantly appointed, it offered a comfortable bed, where Stone slept away the rest of the day and most of the night. Breakfasting early in the hotel dining room, he was joined by a soft-spoken young deputy named Breakenridge.

The young man was happy to hear that Stone's injuries were not serious. He expected Sheriff Behan to return soon with one or all of the bandits in tow. "I wish I could assure you that such incidents are uncommon here, but if they were, we wouldn't need your services. Judge Parker recommended you highly."

Stone asked about the drummer. Breakenridge's humorous handlebars turned down.

"He didn't recover. I came to ask if in view of your unfortunate experience, you'd prefer not to be the man who hangs the culprit."

"I'm not a doctor. There's no conflict."

"Splendid." But there was a slight distaste in the deputy's gentle voice. He apologized for disturbing Stone during his meal and took his leave.

That afternoon, Stone inspected the gallows, built recently of fresh white pine brought in from the Huachuca Mountains expressly for that purpose. It was a more solid construction than he was accustomed to, and had evidently been designed with the anticipation of heavy use. He was testing the trap when a boy in knickerbockers ran up Fourth Street, shouting that the posse had returned with prisoners.

Stone never attended trials, preferring to preserve his neutrality in the interest of a clean and clinical execution. He was forced to make an exception in the case of Tom Glass, the blue-eyed bandit chief accused of stage robbery and complicity in murder, and his partner, Otto Kastler, identified as the man who had searched the passengers and delivered the fatal blow. (A third man, known only as Pidge, had been gunned down by the posse, and two more eluded capture.) As a witness, Stone was summoned to testify. However, on the day he was to appear, Kastler attempted to escape by cracking open Deputy Breakenridge's head with his manacles, and was shot to death by another deputy. The charges of robbery and murder fell on Glass.

The defendant showed no emotion when Stone pointed to him from the witness chair, other than to glare with those eyes of cold fire. They were even more distinctive without the bandanna; Stone got a laugh from the spectators when under cross-examination he told the defense attorney that Glass would have been wiser to cover them and leave his face exposed.

The verdict was swift and lethal. The judge sentenced Glass to hang.

Stone oiled and stretched his ropes, selected one, and appended a hundredweight sack of sand to the end. It shot through the trap with a bang heard throughout Tombstone; certainly in the cell where the condemned man waited. The hangman told the reporter from the *Epitaph* that a specialist who knew his work had no excuse not to deliver sudden, painless death every time; it was all a matter of preparing the rope and proper placement of the knot, severing the spine at the third nuccal vertebra. "A great deal depends, of course, upon height and weight and the condition of the muscles of the neck. Once you've determined those things, you can calculate the drop."

The reporter tugged at his collar and asked how that determination was made.

"With ordinary scales and dressmaker's tape. And with these." Stone held up his hands as if he were about to place them around the reporter's throat. The man did not come back for a second interview.

On the day before the hanging, deputies removed the scales from the Dexter Livery and Feed Stable and set them up in Glass's cell. The prisoner was instructed to step up onto the treadle. When he didn't move, Stone said an accurate figure was necessary to prevent strangulation. Glass paled a shade and complied.

He weighed one hundred seventy-two and a half pounds, with manacles. Stone recorded the information in his pocket notebook, then unrolled his dressmaker's tape, took a quick measurement of the prisoner's height, and wrote five feet, ten inches.

"If you'll allow me." He brought his hands up to Glass's neck.

Glass retreated to the back of the cell. The hatred and horror came back into his eyes. "Tell that strangler to keep his hands off me!"

Deputy Breakenridge, his head still bandaged from the Kastler assault, had lost some of his gentle ways. "I reckon you'll do as your told."

"He's circling, just like a damn buzzard. He's more killer than I am. It was Kastler kilt the drummer."

"The way I heard it, you'd have killed Stone if your pistol didn't misfire."

Stone said, "It will take only a minute. I need to know the strength of your neck."

"I'd let him, Glass. It's to spare you suffering."

"I wisht I'd reloaded them shells myself instead of letting Pidge do it." But he allowed Stone to come forward.

"I've seen men strangle for the ignorance of the hangman," Stone said as he probed the muscles inside Glass's collar. "Their tongues slide out and their faces turn black. Often they soil themselves. That's when the rope is too short and the drop insufficient to snap bone. It's worse the other way. Two years ago in Arizona, a hangman left the rope too long. The fellow was heavy, his neck was weak, and the long drop and the violent stop ripped his head clean off his shoulders. I understand the first two rows of spectators were drenched with blood."

"Get him out of here!" Glass shrieked to Breakenridge.

"It was an unfortunate oversight on the executioner's

part," Stone went on. "Sometimes even an expert can stumble."

"Get him out!"

"Simmer down." Breakenridge unholstered a big Russian revolver and cocked it under the prisoner's chin. "Got what you need, Mr. Stone?"

"I'm finished."

He pocketed his notebook and tape measure and left the cell. All the way down the corridor he heard himself damned in the voice that had read the inscription off the back of his watch.

The hanging was by invitation only. Inside the high board fence that encircled the gallows were gathered the horse-faced editor of the *Epitaph,* two handlebarred men in frock coats representing the city marshal's office, Dr. Matthews with his black bag, and a number of prominent local merchants, who left open an aisle for the prisoner to be escorted to the steps. Stone and Sheriff Behan waited atop the platform as the minister led the procession, droning over an open Bible, followed by Breakenridge and then Glass, with two deputies carrying shotguns behind him. Glass's eyes were startlingly blue in his gray face. Climbing, he missed a step, but recovered his balance with the help of one of the shotgun-toting deputies and continued.

Behan asked the prisoner if he cared to make a valedictory. Glass licked his lips as if to prepare, then shook his head. Stepping forward, Stone slipped the noose over the condemned man's head and snugged the coiled knot into the hollow beneath his left ear; the subaural placement known as the Hangman's Choice. As he did so, his gaze met Glass's. There was no hatred there this time, only horror, and behind it an almost invisible pleading. Stone gave nothing back. He tugged the black hood from his pocket, shook it out, and slid it over Glass's head. He could hear the prisoner's quickened breathing through the dyed cotton.

Stone stepped off the trap and took his place beside the lever. He gripped the polished wooden handle, opened his hand once and closed it again to ensure a firm grasp, and looked at Behan.

The sheriff hesitated, then dipped his head a thousandth of an inch. Stone pulled.

Glass's tall, slender frame appeared to stiffen just before it plummeted through the opening. The rope caught with a bang. Beneath it, inaudible to all but the hangman, came the splintering crackle of the spine severing at the third nuccal vertebra.

As Dr. Matthews ducked under the platform, Stone didn't wait for him to announce that Glass had died instantaneously. He descended the steps, followed the path made for him by the spectators, and let himself out through the gate in the fence.

Copyrights and Permissions